THE POWER OF POETRY

Teen Verse

Edited By Briony Kearney

First published in Great Britain in 2023 by:

Young Writers
Remus House
Coltsfoot Drive
Peterborough
PE2 9BF
Telephone: 01733 890066
Website: www.youngwriters.co.uk

All Rights Reserved
Book Design by Ashley Janson
© Copyright Contributors 2023
Softback ISBN 978-1-80459-600-5

Printed and bound in the UK by BookPrintingUK
Website: www.bookprintinguk.com
YB0545P

FOREWORD

Since 1991, here at Young Writers we have celebrated the awesome power of creative writing, especially in young adults where it can serve as a vital method of expressing their emotions and views about the world around them. In every poem we see the effort and thought that each student published in this book has put into their work and by creating this anthology we hope to encourage them further with the ultimate goal of sparking a life-long love of writing.

Our latest competition for secondary school students, **The Power of Poetry,** challenged young writers to consider what was important to them and how to express that using the power of words. We wanted to give them a voice, the chance to express themselves freely and honestly, something which is so important for these young adults to feel confident and listened to. They could give an opinion, highlight an issue, consider a dilemma, impart advice or simply write about something they love. There were no restrictions on style or subject so you will find an anthology brimming with a variety of poetic styles and topics. We hope you find it as absorbing as we have.

We encourage young writers to express themselves and address subjects that matter to them, which sometimes means writing about sensitive or contentious topics. If you have been affected by any issues raised in this book, details on where to find help can be found at
www.youngwriters.co.uk/info/other/contact-lines

CONTENTS

Clacton County High School, Clacton-On-Sea

Luke Roberts (11)	1
Jake Batchelor (15)	2
Athena Mandelenis (14)	4
Ellie Singers (13)	6
Lola Collins (12)	8
Angel San Jose (11)	10
Dan Faint (15)	12
A Connor Sutherley (15)	14
Freja Turner-Butler (14)	15
Katie French (13)	16
Kelsey Gray	18
Kane Steele (12)	19
Christopher Harris (12)	20
Lara Predescu (12)	21
April Aghoghovbia (11)	22
Scarlet Cooper (13)	23
Ava Mae Renaut (12)	24
Lillie Argent (14)	25
Maisey Dearsley (11)	26
Maisie Pryke (11)	27
Charlie Chisnall (12)	28
Daisy Ollivant (12)	29
Chloe Pickard (12)	30
Moyin Olufajo (14)	31
Taylor Douglas (11)	32
Harrison Fox (11)	33
Leah Tully (12)	34
Victor Madro (11)	35

Sandymoor Ormiston Academy, Sandymoor

Rianne Boelema (13)	36
Lydia Allan (11)	37
Joshua Myers	38
Jessica Lowe (13)	40
Jacob Simpson (12)	41
Finlay Downey (12)	42
Kieran Berry (12)	43
Sandra Klepets (13)	44
Isobel Hall (12)	45
Adam Kurzec (12)	46
Mia Jackson (12)	47
Alyssa Asgill (12)	48
Sam Gilfoyle (11)	49
Harley Langley	50
Maisy Shorrock (12)	51
Anabel Story (12)	52
Millie Stringer (12)	53
Kate Barlow (12)	54
Chloe Tinsley (12)	55
Josh Baldock (11)	56
Neasa Hughes (12)	57
Jenson Tildsley (12)	58
Holly Talbot (12)	59
Anastasia Procek (12)	60
Calvin Roberts (11)	61
Finlay Pitcher (12)	62
Holly Tasker (12)	63
Mouamen Ashour (12)	64
Mia O'Mahoney (13)	65
Charly Fuller (12)	66
Oliver Baskeyfield (12)	67
Hari Owen (11)	68
Jack Rogers (12)	69

Jeremiasz Krawczyk (12)	70
Ben Brizell (13)	71
Nikola Lewandowska (13)	72
Ellie Costigan (13)	73
Luke Keenan (12)	74
Kristofer Klepets (11)	75
Daniel Jones (12)	76
Jack James (12)	77
Harry Simpson (12)	78
Jack Metcalfe (13)	79
Bethany Dimelow (13)	80
Maya Hanson (12)	81
Harry Huby (13)	82
Finlay Mason (12)	83
Dylan Faragher (11)	84
Joe Fahimi (12)	85
Josh Totten (12)	86
Corey Birch-McClure (12)	87
Liam O'Connell (12)	88
Pippa Smith-Cole (12)	89
Harrison Shingler (12)	90

St Pius X Catholic High School, Wath Upon Dearne

Rithika Raj (11)	91
Joshua Griffiths (13)	92
Elodia Stanley (11)	94
Emilia Cichy (13)	96
Elodia Stanley (11)	98
Danielle Lukey (15)	100
Christopher Reading	101
Maja Wegrzyn (11)	102
Ebony Bull (11)	103
Isabelle Leary (13)	104
Joe Ellis (11)	105
Max Gumienny (12)	106
Alexi Hague (12)	107
Patrik Krajci (13)	108
Jack Wigley (12)	109
Zack Foster (11)	110
Harvey Roy Dennis Penrose (12)	111
Safiya Kettlewell (13)	112
Isaac Law (12)	113

Charlie Tracy-Taylor (12)	114
Elliott Hanson (11)	115
Prada Bates (11)	116
Dillon Kitchen (11)	117
Harriet Allen (13)	118
Lily Towlerton (12)	119
Ava Poole (11)	120
Louisa Nayar (11)	121
Jaiden Hill (11)	122
Isaac Garrett (11)	123
Yuliia Rohach (11)	124
Julia Moyo (13)	125

Vyners School, Ickenham

Ibrahim Khalid (11)	126
Parth Joshi (12)	129
Ali Mansoor (15)	130
Bradley Stilwell (11)	133
Nevaeh Aaliyah Aulakh (12)	134
Natasha Islentsyeva (11)	136
Ava Queenan (11)	138
Bobbie Sleet (11)	140
Ruby Farrington (13)	141
Amelie Wootton (12)	142
Sienna Kaur Gill (14)	143
Shaza Nusrath (15)	144
Muhammad Umar Zahid (11)	145
Sophie Hawkins (12)	146
Shawn Gera (12)	147
Ibrahim Ramzan (11)	148
Dejonique Wilson (11)	149
Raphael Belai (15)	150
Catherine Gallagher (12)	151
Juliet Marshall (14)	152
Kyle Kohli (12)	153
Zara Colyer (12)	154
Daniel Hassanian (15)	155
Tejpal Chanonia (15)	156
Holly Canovas (12)	157
Khwaish Pandya (11)	158
Archie Greenan (11)	159
Amber Wong (14)	160
Daniyal Dossa (11)	161

Matthew Parker (11)	162
Munira Khan (11)	163
Leonardo Sawden (12)	164
Georgina Francis (12)	165
Deven Daurka (11)	166
Nathan Betts (12)	167
Yara Imad (15)	168
Valentina Cossio-Yates (15)	169
Celina Bandera Villaescusa (12)	170
Ayrton Rai (12)	171
Nally Aziz (12)	172
Sophia Monk (12)	173
Aidan Jones (11)	174
Alexander Baughan (11)	175
Michele Cronin (11)	176
Haitao Liang (11)	177
Zoher Alkhouli (12)	178
Amelia Baah (12)	179
Luca Harrod (12)	180
Aaron Rashid (12)	181
Harvey Matharu (11)	182
Layo Oluyemi (11)	183
Fleur Wright (12)	184
Matthew Burke (12)	185
Aaryan Thakrar (12)	186
Daniel Gavin (11)	187
Harry Deanus (11)	188
Sleiman Basma (11)	189

THE POEMS

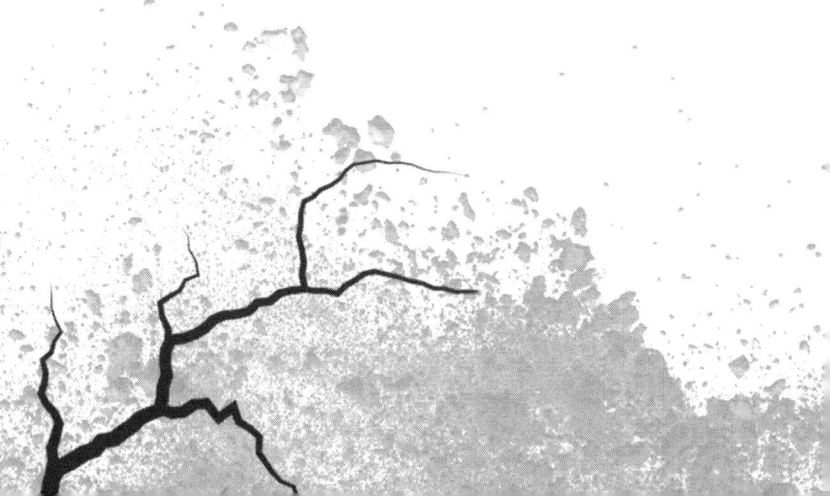

Q And Queer

Another cry, another shout,
Another plea and it's about
These other jokes, these other lies,
These other jeers, we have no more tries,
'You stopped the fire, saved coal-burnt skin,
But you still commit to this ancient sin,

Woman and woman, man and man,
I think it's time we came up with a plan
To end all evil's glory days,
To stop bis, lezers and gays',

Why think it's a joke when it's what we live?
Our romance that you can't forgive,
Why try when you'll just shoot us down?
And strip us of our rainbow crown,
Why bully us for who we are?
To be cut short, unable to go far,

We fight for justice, we fight for truth,
But kicked out, we are, from your roof,
We cry for answers, we cry for rights,
But why don't we get it? Only one more fight.

Luke Roberts (11)
Clacton County High School, Clacton-On-Sea

Memories

Bullets whistling past me,
flying past the bushes and trees.
Someone brushed past me,
suddenly, I heard squelching mud,
followed by a thundering thud.
Flash.

And here we are, back in time,
when everyone could hear bells chime.
Children were running around to play,
but obviously, that was back in the day.

Conflict. Peace. What is the difference?
Conflict. A place of war and loss,
with families praying at the cross.
Peace. Clear skies and not a worry,
no one rushing, panicking, in a hurry.
So why?

What is this about Russia and Ukraine?
All of these soldiers suffering in pain,
and families are forced to flee home.
A place to make you feel safe,
can only talk to loved ones on the phone,
but phones don't help with faith.

So please, stop this, it is not right,
if affects others, not just the ones in the fight.
Flash.

I am back again, stuck in the past,
oh, the days I got put in a cast,
instead of being in these refined beds,
laying there while I helplessly bled.

War and conflict have to end,
country relations need a little mend.
People do not need to get killed,
imagine all our soldiers coming home safely,
all families' hearts would be filled.
Bullets whistling past me.

So here we are again,
trenches, memories, friends,
all united, not in the same place,
not from when we laughed face-to-face.
I feared this day.
The day that God came to take you away,

I beg, please, don't leave without me.
I will get down on one knee
and beg for eternal mercy.

Jake Batchelor (15)
Clacton County High School, Clacton-On-Sea

Amber Rays

Amber rays shine on my wake,
A blinding, joyful fortress, like
Pillar of stone, they rumble;
A near-joy scrambled
And scattered beautifully.
Take a lake, if you will,
A flowing life, walled
And caged, but flowing,
Controlled, tempered,
Alive.

Amber rays shine on my day,
A blinding, calming fortress, why
Do all not feel gratitude and splendour
For grand Kore of Auxerre?
An archaic smile, devoid of devotion.
Take this lady, if you will,
A flowing life, captured
In stone, but flowing,
Controlled, tempered,
Remembered.

Amber rays strike on this night,
A blinding, enclosing fortress, spikes
Grow on the backs of snakes, disguised.
Credence requires little testament, the wise

and foolish dare not ask,
they do not dare heed.
Take Medusa, if you will,
Once a life, cut short
And drained, no longer flowing,
Controlled, deceived,
Dead.

Amber rays die on this day,
No longer blinding, but clear to me.
Streaks of shattered hope, a scene
Only for me, others are all blinded still.
Only I testify, only I defy known credence,
Now a baseline, once thought a novelty, when
And why does power equal
Artistic, social status? Take the fallen angel,
If you will, which you must,
A flowing life, mocked
And shamed, but flowing,
Unashamed, ferocious,
Free.

Athena Mandelenis (14)
Clacton County High School, Clacton-On-Sea

Summer Has Come Again

It's summer soon and everyone is buzzing,
Ice pops and watermelons,
Lemons and cake,

It's summer soon and the sun is out,
The hot days and the shiny, sunny sun,
Crop tops and shorts,
Shaving your legs,
That's just what summer is,

All the days to lie in bed,
All the day to do nothing at all,
That's just what summer is,

Summer is like Christmas,
You can't wait for summer to start,

It's time to go outside,
Sunbathe by the pool,
Skating down by the pier,
Playing pranks on your sibling,
That's just what summer is,

Summer is the best season,
You have time off school,
The Olympics are held,
Waterparks are open,
That's just what summer is,

20th June makes you want to jump with joy,
But 20th September makes you want to cry with sadness,
94 days of summer is just not enough,

Thunderstorms at night,
The sun shining the next,
The moon is full and the stars are bright,
That's just what summer is,

It's summer soon and everyone is buzzing,
Sitting on the beach,
Feeding the ducks,
Walking in the woods,
Swimming in the pool,
Cartwheeling down the hill,
Going to the park,
That's just what summer is.

Ellie Singers (13)
Clacton County High School, Clacton-On-Sea

In What World Is It Okay To Target Children?

Strangers may not be as nice as they seem,
So if you are scared, it's okay to scream,
Don't get in a stranger's car,
So stick to these rules, wherever you are,
Your door might go ring-a-ding-ding,
But don't let them in,
They say they're fourteen,
But they're really forty,
Online websites are as scary as in real life,
Stay safe online,
Sharing personal information isn't fine,
Don't agree to meet up with strangers,
There are scary places
Where they tell you to go,
But you really don't know,
Not everyone is bad, but listen to me when I say this:
The world is a very dangerous place,
We don't know who we can trust,
But I believe we can stop this,
We need to!
For people's own safety,
It could be your child that goes missing,
Your family member,

It could be anyone,
We need to make this world safe,
Because at the moment, it's not,
Let's fight for the future,
Fight for our lives,
Let's make this world safer.

Lola Collins (12)
Clacton County High School, Clacton-On-Sea

Who Exactly Are You?

A girl was standing in front of me,
she was a girl from my class,
but who was she, exactly?
I didn't really know who she was,
it was as if she was a ghost, invisible to the world.
Until I realised, I'd known her this whole time,
the girl who resembled the sun,
bright and full of elation that sparkled in her eyes.
The girl who would walk home,
being discriminated and hated for being who she was.
Was it because of her hair?
Or was it because she's Asian?
A different race from everyone else,
if that was the case,
in a society where they've never seen someone
with slanted eyes or gradients of brown.
Why must she change herself?
Was there any need?
Her laugh was like her friend's,
and her smile was like her mum's,
it would always resemble other people,
but not herself.
However, deep down, somewhere hidden,

I knew that hopeless girl
in the mirror
was none other than myself.

Angel San Jose (11)
Clacton County High School, Clacton-On-Sea

Stamford Bridge Is The Place To Be

Football is pain, football is joy,
Football is for girls, football is for boys,
I love football, it's so fun,
But when Chelsea lose, I pull out a gun,
Football means the world to me,
You see,
Kick the ball in the net,
Score a goal, you're a threat,

The crowd to me,
The people you see,
From girls to boys,
Men to women,
Then a goal is scored,
The crowd roars,
A special place to me,
Come with, you will see,
Stamford Bridge, what a sight to see,
90 minutes gone, extra time now,
squeaky bum time.

This game is so fun,
Out of nowhere, an attack gone wrong,
Mount with the ball, he's attacking,
Turned around, now play's reversing,
Back around we go now, we're traversing
travella Pass, now we're talking,
90+3, a minute to be,
Ball goes through, scores the goal,
Stamford Bridge is the place to be.

Dan Faint (15)
Clacton County High School, Clacton-On-Sea

Camera, Action

He treats me like his wife,
He calls me names,
He holds my hand and hurts me in private,
He holds me by the waist,
He takes me everywhere and protects me,
He defends my innocence and youth,
That's what he likes, he finds it cute,
He treats me like his wife,
As he drives, he slides over his hand,
And puts it on my thigh,
He orders me around, insulting everything of mine,
And yet I'm still like a wife,
He curses and spits,
Every tight thing has to fit,
His verses of narcissism,
It's all behind the camera, a glorified prison,
It all goes down, like the hand against my backside,
Especially if you don't defend him or pretend to be happy,
Even in the end, run from his frustrated strides,
I'm still like his wife.

A Connor Sutherley (15)
Clacton County High School, Clacton-On-Sea

Complaints

Every cloud has a silver lining,
Yet sometimes it's hard to find,
Every scar has a story,
Yet most are never told,
Every problem has a solution,
Yet some problems aren't solved,
If you took the time to look for meaning,
You'd complain your time's been wasted,
Yet we complain the days are too long,
There isn't any meaning for it,
If you had the confidence to do it, you would,
But it takes effort to have confidence,
Yet if you were just handed it,
You'd say it's too easy,
Most of life is spent complaining
About things it's a privilege to have,
So, instead of worrying why's this and why's that,
Go claim that advantage,
Before you lose the chance.

Freja Turner-Butler (14)
Clacton County High School, Clacton-On-Sea

Do I Fit In?

New school,
Mum says it will be fun,
I say, not cool,
School is far, I have to run,
Apparently, I can learn,
But I think I will crash and burn.

The uniform looks trash,
I hope the lights don't flash,
The boys are rough,
But I am not tough.

Do I have to be like them?
I don't want to drown in the River Thames,
I hope the teachers are nice,
And I don't catch lice.

All this makes me wonder,
Will I be strong like thunder?

They might think I'm dumb,
Then I will be numb,
Forget the bad,
Think of the good.

They could like me,
And protect me from a bee,
If I become smart,
I will bake a tart,
We are all wearing the same,
I hope I'm not lame.

Katie French (13)
Clacton County High School, Clacton-On-Sea

My Frustrations

In the world, there's violence,
and there are children out there
who are dying.
There's pollution out there,
but people can't make a solution.

Plastic spreading, it just stretches
like elastic.
I don't want the world like this,
it feels like we are stuck
in this terrible environment.

People litter,
that's so bitter.
All the poor innocent animals
crying with a roar
when they die and choke on plastic.

The world needs to change,
like now,
it makes me nervous and worried,
how cruel people treat
my surroundings.
Fix this world!

Kelsey Gray
Clacton County High School, Clacton-On-Sea

Save Our Planet

Save our planet,
Use paper, not plastic,
Think of the next generation having fun,
We will have had so much fun,
But they will not,
No healthy sea,
No animals,
Nothing,
So please be considerate,
Save our planet!
And stop pollution,
And forest fires,
There are animals that die and go extinct
Because of cars,
So avoid them as much as you can,
Motorbikes, cars, buses, taxis,
All cause it,
Animals dying so we can eat meat,
Why not eat a bit of food, but not meat?
Think of all the animals that would still be alive,
If us greedy humans weren't so selfish.

Kane Steele (12)
Clacton County High School, Clacton-On-Sea

Help Us Stop This Once And For All

Hi, my name is Christopher,
Or Chris for short,
Can I ask you a question?
Okay, so, basically,
people around the world and in the UK
are being bullied,
especially people who are black.
People get called names,
some people go past these names
and don't listen to them,
but some can't.
They get bullied every day,
every week, every month,
whether that is following them home,
or doing it online.
So please, I will stop this
'til this is finished across the world,
saying, No More Racism.
So will you help me?
Thank you for your time.

Christopher Harris (12)
Clacton County High School, Clacton-On-Sea

Making A Difference Today

I want to be a blessing to you.
With all my strength, I can give it to you,
I can offer a ride, a penny or two,
To make you smile, please don't be blue.

I can send you a card, a gift, a call,
So that you will be standing tall,
I will give you the best today,
And make a difference for you to stay.

So light up that somber side,
There is always a light that never hides,
God will always be there for you,
And so will my hugs, to keep you through.

Smile and the world will smile back at you,
And make a difference for me and you.

Lara Predescu (12)
Clacton County High School, Clacton-On-Sea

Zero To Hero

Words can hurt, they can shoot you down in pain,
Some to make others think they're insane,
A hurricane of emotions, twirling in your head,
The words making you want to run away, home to your bed,
Lie there hearing drip, drip, drip,
And the clock tick, tock, tick,
An endless fall, don't you know this will upset her?
The real truth is she is better,
She is better than your unkind lies,
It hurts others inside, realise,
We are trying to heal negative minds,
And let's stop bullying, please, for our mankind.

April Aghoghovbia (11)
Clacton County High School, Clacton-On-Sea

Soil And Gold

Gold blocks glistening in the sun,
As bright as a star,
Soil out in the cold,
Wishing to have fun.

Fuel runs free in a gold mine's factory,
While soil's roots run dry,
Gold blocks shine bright,
Even in the darkness of night.

While grainy skin of soil
Lives in an environment where things are tight.

Soil just wants to be clean,
Washed in soap, self-esteem and copper,
Gold needs a flash to reality,
Because the value of equality
Is worth more than the value of money.

Scarlet Cooper (13)
Clacton County High School, Clacton-On-Sea

We All Have The Same Human Rights

However different we are,
we should always be treated the same,
girl, boy, fat, skinny, brown, gay,
we're all the same.
Treat us right and let us be,
it doesn't matter how we look,
or how we speak,
treat us right and let us be.
We need to put a stop to this,
it's mean and selfish,
it's horrible and rude,
let us have our rights.
We don't need to be the same,
just end this rudeness,
and treat us right.
Let us be,
it doesn't matter how we look or speak.

Ava Mae Renaut (12)
Clacton County High School, Clacton-On-Sea

Different In A Good Way

My name is my identity,
But my behaviour does not define me,
Once you get to know me,
You might end up liking me.

Every day is a struggle,
Normal daily tasks get in a muddle,
The frustration and anger can build up inside,
This is how I deal with things, it builds up and I cry.

On my own, I sit and play,
Not mixing with other children throughout the day,
I may be different, but I want to be liked,
I may never get there, but I'll try to be nice.

Lillie Argent (14)
Clacton County High School, Clacton-On-Sea

Shaming

You may shame me for who I am,
Glaring at me like I'm different,
But I am a human too,
Just like you.

You said to me,
"You're just a woman."
But I am a human too,
Just like you.

Sexism spreading like a germ,
They need to learn,
"You can't, you're just a girl."
"Your favourite colour is pink."
But this needs to stop,
Once and for all.

Maisey Dearsley (11)
Clacton County High School, Clacton-On-Sea

The Bullies

It's a school day and
you make it through half of the day.
Sit down at the lunch table,
eating with your friends,
they leave.
There's a boy staring at you,
he comes closer,
pushes you on the floor
and snatches your keys.
You get up to grab them
but he's teasing you,
hiding the keys up high
above your reach.
At this point, everyone's laughing
like a pack of hyenas.

Maisie Pryke (11)
Clacton County High School, Clacton-On-Sea

Curious Disease

My disease is getting worse and worse,
you have seen me since I was born,
and you have caught me out.

I am dying because of my disease,
there is no cure,
but I would sacrifice anything
to go outside to the real world
before I die.

Please, if anyone can hear,
like a god or anyone,
please get a cure for me,
and I shall worship you,
and do anything for you,
and thank you.

Charlie Chisnall (12)
Clacton County High School, Clacton-On-Sea

Our World Is Changing

Roses are red,
Violets are blue,
The world is changing,
And we are too.

The skies are grey,
And cold,
People lay on our streets,
And political problems start.

Strikes start,
And our world is crumbling,
People are dying.

Our world is changing,
Happier lives, we used to have,
Turned grey and dark,
Positivity is dying,
Life is dull.

Daisy Ollivant (12)
Clacton County High School, Clacton-On-Sea

Wildlife

W hat will we do if we keep on using plastic?
I f the wildlife goes, it won't be the same,
L ife is important to animals, bees create honey,
D epends on you to save wildlife,
L ife is important to you and animals,
I s it fun to keep on using plastic?
F ish die because of plastic,
E very animal and all wildlife matters to us.

Chloe Pickard (12)
Clacton County High School, Clacton-On-Sea

Living At A Cost

The cost of living,
Living at a cost,
Working to live,
In a system where you have to live to work,
Whatever meaning your life had,
Covered in over-priced products,
And gas costs,
Didn't ask to live, but paying the price,
A price you can't afford,
And all these politics make me bored,
Tired of living at a cost,
And I don't want to pay anymore.

Moyin Olufajo (14)
Clacton County High School, Clacton-On-Sea

Oceans And Seas

I believe we can stop throwing rubbish in the sea,
We can see the dirty water, or even the rivers,
I believe,

I believe you can see the colour of the sea,
Brown, green, or even all the rubbish,
I believe,

Can you see what I see?
All the rubbish in the ocean or the sea,
Just like me, I believe, I believe, I believe.

Taylor Douglas (11)
Clacton County High School, Clacton-On-Sea

The Future

Don't look back at yesterday,
Or what you have left behind,
For only the future is now your aim,
And your best moment will always be your favourite.

Today is the day you become you,
Think about memories, not nightmares,
You only have one soul, save it for the best,
You are the future of you, not other people.

Harrison Fox (11)
Clacton County High School, Clacton-On-Sea

The Environment

I just want to say that
every time I go to the beach,
trashed.
Every time I go to the park,
it's all trashed.
So I just need to say,
you need to stop
throwing trash in the ocean,
the beach,
the park,
and the sidewalk.
Just recycle it,
and then the world
will become even better.

Leah Tully (12)
Clacton County High School, Clacton-On-Sea

Don't Waste

Waste, taste,
Share, care,
Give, don't waste food,
Just be a cool dude,
If you waste,
Poor people will never taste,
If you give food,
You'll be a cool dude,
Be nice,
So homeless people will get rice,
Don't waste food,
And you'll be a cool dude.

Victor Madro (11)
Clacton County High School, Clacton-On-Sea

Colours And Sheep

I am a black sheep,
Living in a world that was not made for me,
I can't say a peep,
The white sheep rule,
And sit and drool,
No other colour sheep has been in charge,
Not pink or yellow or even royal blue,

Every summer, the white sheep are sheared,
While every other colour sit and peer,
But in the winter, every other colour if sheared,
Leaving us cold and in fear,

And if one of us wants different-coloured wool,
The ruling sheep make us feel dull,
And if we like the same-coloured sheep,
We are made to weep,

The little lambs are taught how to jump and fly,
But if we left them on their own, they may die,
They should be taught how to eat grass,
And taught how to not pass,

And if you think white sheep are less dangerous than black sheep,
Then you are clearly amiss,
White sheep are the ones causing harm,
But in the end, our wool is being made into yarn.

Rianne Boelema (13)
Sandymoor Ormiston Academy, Sandymoor

Bullying Should Be Banned

Bullying is a problem, it's been around forever,
But still, nobody has been able to change it completely for the better,
It's something, it's there, it happens every day,
But still, nobody has been able to make it go away,
Just sit back and think, has it ever happened to you?
I know it's hard, but there's something you can do,
Stand up, speak up, don't just sit and dwell,
For I have a solution, it should make things go well,
Read these words then go away,
Follow it and you might have a better day,
Tell your grandpa, grandma, or your mum and dad,
Once you've done that, what can go bad?
They'll help you, I'm sure,
Speak up, that should be law,
But now we're here and I have a mission for you,
It's really, really simple, it's not much to do,
Only say kind things, think before you speak,
And that, my friends, is it from me!

Lydia Allan (11)
Sandymoor Ormiston Academy, Sandymoor

World War

World war is melancholy,
the destruction and death,
the loss of those you know.
Bang. Bang. Bang!
As their final breath lasts on Earth.
People hiding in the trenches.
March. March. March!
To the next town, they go,
no person can debate,
this was not great.
The killings and explosions
dotted around,
our own species
killing one another.
Then, in quick action,
the victor comes out.
The PTSD and fear in their eyes,
rather traumatised.
However, the respect we shall give,
forever and ever,
saving our lives.
Even today, war carries on.
The unfairness of those
who died for war to stop,
just so we carry on.

God bless those soldiers
and innocent people
who died.
I only hope there is never
that day where our world
fights again.

Joshua Myers
Sandymoor Ormiston Academy, Sandymoor

Ode To Football

Oh, football, oh, football, oh, it's so fun,
Some people call it soccer, but that's just dumb,
It helps you get outside,
Instead of being on your backside.

Oh, football, oh, football, it's not just for fun,
You can even get your anger out
By booting the ball,
Even if your team hasn't won.

Oh, football, oh, football, some people say it's bad,
Because you could get hurt,
But you just need to grow up and be a lad,
Don't be sad,
A motto I live off, which isn't that bad,
Is you have to feel the pain to win the game.

Oh, football, oh, football, it's just so fun,
You bring people as a team,
And nobody is mean,
You try your best, even if you don't succeed,
Football is the thing you really need.

Jessica Lowe (13)
Sandymoor Ormiston Academy, Sandymoor

Dogs Are The Best Pets In The World

Dogs are the best pets in the world,
They are so helpful, I love them,
They love our company and we love theirs,
We need to have dogs everywhere.

Dogs make life fun from start to end,
There's a reason they're known as man's best friend,
They run so fast as a frisbee is hurled,
Dogs are the best pets in the world.

You might think cats are easier to own,
But dogs are friendlier and they stay at home,
I get it, cats can be nice, but
Dogs are the best pets in the world.

Dogs are great with kids and they're really entertaining,
They're always happy, even when it's raining,
They're so funny, I don't know what we'd do without them,
Dogs are the best pets in the world.

Jacob Simpson (12)
Sandymoor Ormiston Academy, Sandymoor

Swim All Day Long

Look at the calm waves in the pool,
Oh, how I love to swim in the pool,
Feeling the waves splash around me,
But they can be violent, which I hate to see,
Floating and bobbing all around,
Breathing slowly and not making a sound,
Even though there are swimmers nearby,
Splashing and kicking, but they pass by,
Maybe get bored and do a couple of tricks,
But if you're doing flips, make sure you don't get sick,
Whether it's sitting on the ground,
Or doing a swim like a worm, you can have fun all around,
When you have your head underwater,
All you can hear is the lovely sound of calm water,
Look at the calm waves in the pool,
I think swimming is the best hobby,
I hope you love it too, just as much as me.

Finlay Downey (12)
Sandymoor Ormiston Academy, Sandymoor

Knife Crime

Knife crime should be stopped,
I'm here to tell you what it's about,
Just to put out a bit of a shout,
Knife crime should be stopped.

This crime is one of the worst,
As it could happen from a drug bust,
As it could be done to anyone,
But knife crime should never be done,
Knife crime should be stopped.

Some people use it for revenge,
Some people use it to scare people,
But either way, both are dull,
As it should never be done,
Knife crime should be stopped.

Knife crime almost happened to someone I know,
But it should not happen to any foe,
As it could be from racism or appearance,
But no one should go through this hell dance,
Knife crime must be stopped.

Kieran Berry (12)
Sandymoor Ormiston Academy, Sandymoor

Anti-Poetry

I do not like poetry,
It takes up a lot of time,
It is impossible to make it rhyme,
And I always struggle on the last line.

When English rolls around,
A poem, we are told to write,
Mine always ends up looking a sight,
And reading it back always gives me a fright.

I do not like poetry,
It is such a bore,
It should be against the law,
And it makes me feel hatred to my core.

My time is better spent on something worth it,
While I spend hours writing as I sit,
I could solve world hunger,
Who would have thought it?

I do not like poetry,
I will not read it,
I will not enjoy it,
And I will never, ever write it.

I do not like poetry!

Sandra Klepets (13)
Sandymoor Ormiston Academy, Sandymoor

Just A Game?

Horror games are thrilling,
Dramatically killing,
Hiding in a bush,
Covering up sounds with a toilet flush,

The classic 'run but you can't hide',
I know the murderer tried,
Through the wind and snow,
Little do they know,

I escaped that horrible place,
And solved the case
Of the boy that went missing,
On the day, everyone was listening,

Turning on the news,
Hearing the boos,
Crying in caves,
The boy wasn't so brave,

With a slash of a knife of his neck,
People went on a long trek,
Only to find
The boy dead behind
The lamppost where he went missing,

But it's only a game,
Right?

Isobel Hall (12)
Sandymoor Ormiston Academy, Sandymoor

The Lord Almighty

The Lord has given you everything,
Everything that you and I can see,
Fish, cows, grass, flowers and soil,
Monkeys, trees, birds, you and me,
Snakes, rice fields, cats, sheep and bogs,
Dragonflies, toads, goats, cotton and hills,
Ice, snow, rain, sky, and the seven seas,
Now, there have been times you weren't grateful,
And that means you have sinned,
But that's okay, you can be forgiven,
The Lord almighty, He will forgive you,
Every day and night, to the Lord, I pray,
I pray for good for me, my family, and the world,
Sometimes, if I have time,
I read the Lord's word,
God will protect the women and the men,
Through Christ, our Lord,
Amen.

Adam Kurzec (12)
Sandymoor Ormiston Academy, Sandymoor

Girls Are Good At Football

Girls are good at football,
While it may not seem true,
Just give them a ball and a wall,
And watch what they can do.

Women's football is underrated,
They have been neglected a few times too many,
I think more of it should be appreciated,
To support them costs less than a penny.

Women's football continues to grow,
When people come to watch the game,
And as fans fill up, row upon row,
More people get to know its name.

But here is one thing I know for a fact,
And this is a thing where we can all make a pact,
That no matter what ethnicity, sexuality, or race,
People always get brought together by the game's grace.

Mia Jackson (12)
Sandymoor Ormiston Academy, Sandymoor

The Night

The night, as calming as the crashing waves,
The most quiet part of all my days,
At night, you are as free as can be,
It's the most gorgeous thing that you can see.

The night, as calming as the crackling fire,
Skies so dark, you will be inspired,
In the darkness of the night, nature comes alive,
At night, nature really starts to thrive.

The night, as cold as the freezing ice,
It's dangerous and cold, that's not nice,
Night is the time when your head hits the pillow,
Night is when your brain turns to jello.

The night, as dark as a black cat's fur,
When the sun rises, you enter a nightmare.

Alyssa Asgill (12)
Sandymoor Ormiston Academy, Sandymoor

Football Is Fabulous

You often wake up early,
You'll have to set an alarm,
Despite footballers diving,
Don't copy and keep on thriving.

Many can be very rough,
Go to the gym and get tough,
Brazilians do their samba dance,
Don't get angry, it's just bants.

Football has a lot of passion,
It's just a kit, not fashion,
Make sure to wear your shinpads,
Or you could get injured by the aggressive lads.

Argentina won the World Cup in December,
Lionel Messi was the core member,
Cristiano Ronaldo, Messi's closest competition,
Unfortunately, Ronaldo couldn't complete the number one mission.

Sam Gilfoyle (11)
Sandymoor Ormiston Academy, Sandymoor

Football Is The Best Hobby

It brings people together,
It makes people competitive,
It makes people show their true colours,
It is a therapy, it makes your adrenaline pump.

Some people may say it brings
Racism, hate, greed, vandalism, panic, your heart sinks,
You can lose again and again,
You can get bullied for your team losing, even though it's not your fault.

It also brings
Joy, excitement, heartbreak, makes your adrenaline rush,
It also shows kindness in the players' hearts,
It shows respect and ambition,
It shows players fighting for the badge and for the win,
It shows people supporting as if their lives depend on it.

Harley Langley
Sandymoor Ormiston Academy, Sandymoor

Me And Bertie

My favourite horse is called Bertie,
His favourite fruit has to be cherry,
Without his rug, he gets a little cold,
Without his rug, he goes for a roll.

Some may say it is dangerous and cruel,
But there is only love, it's my number one rule,
I may fall and he may trip, meaning to take a break,
When he's ready, his tricks we remake.

Bertie can be difficult, following instructions,
But he is well-behaved when we do our productions,
Jumping is his favourite thing to do,
Although he spooks when he hears a moo.

Bertie has taught me to appreciate,
More memories that we will create.

Maisy Shorrock (12)
Sandymoor Ormiston Academy, Sandymoor

On Holiday Is My Favourite Place To Be

On holiday is my favourite place to be,
Sitting by the pool is all I want to see,
Blanketed by the sun,
Hoping this dream will never be done.

On holiday is my favourite place to be,
Walking in the hot weather, feeling free,
The breakfast starts the day like no other food could,
And treats you like any other breakfast should.

Some say it's not worth the cost,
But look at the happiness they have lost,
Walking back into the airport,
Leaves me feeling distraught.

Getting back on the plane,
I know I'm home when I see the rain,
On holiday is my favourite place to be.

Anabel Story (12)
Sandymoor Ormiston Academy, Sandymoor

The Dying Flower

This child is an orphan who cries to sleep,
She is like a lovely dying flower,
My flower is lonely, no hope she keeps,
She is hungry, thirsty, losing power.

Every time I see her, I want to cry,
If only I could help her along,
Depressed, anxious, grieving, and very dry,
My flower weeps because of her really sad song.

One day, my flower wakes up to start afresh,
I begin to think there may be some hope,
Population caused her family to stress,
So she's alone now to make a new scope.

My flower thought this was to be the end,
But, at last, she smiles with all of her friends.

Millie Stringer (12)
Sandymoor Ormiston Academy, Sandymoor

Going On Holiday

Going on holiday is my favourite thing to do,
Swimming in the sea, so beautiful and blue,
Sunbathing on the golden sand and eating ice cream,
Going to the beach and feeling supreme.

Going on holiday is the best,
Sitting by the pool and having a rest,
Spending time with family and friends,
The excitement and joy will never end.

Going on holiday is very fun,
Eating delicious food underneath the sun,
Going to a restaurant for family dinner,
Eating all my food and feeling like a winner.

Going on holiday is my favourite thing to do,
So I hope that you enjoy it too.

Kate Barlow (12)
Sandymoor Ormiston Academy, Sandymoor

Cats Versus Dogs

Cats are a lot better than dogs,
Where dogs are messy, big, and loud,
Cats are quiet, and fluffy as a cloud,
Dogs need attention 24/7,
But cats are angels sent from heaven.

Cats are a lot better than dogs,
Dogs are messy and cost a lot of money,
But cats are clean and act so funny,
Cats are affectionate and always show love,
Where dogs can be violent and sometimes shove.

Cats are a lot better than dogs,
Where cats are independent and so tidy,
Dogs are high-maintenance and often act wildly,
Dogs have way too much energy,
But cats are calm and tranquil as the sea.

Chloe Tinsley (12)
Sandymoor Ormiston Academy, Sandymoor

2023

Oh, dang, it's 2023,
New year, new me,
And last year wasn't easy,

Over in Ukraine,
Russian bullets rain,
Climate change,
The whole world is going to heal,
But that doesn't mean
We can't change ourselves,

The Ukrainians pray,
So the lurking soldiers will go away,
And I'm just here to say
That we need to fight
For what we share,
Stop the environment's doom,
That is climate change
Knocking on our door,

Yes, it's 2023,
And I hope this year is filled with glee,
To make sure that we set the world free.

Josh Baldock (11)
Sandymoor Ormiston Academy, Sandymoor

Why You Should Read

A book is like a roller coaster,
With highs and lows,
Sometimes happy, sometimes sad,
Scary parts and mad,
Then those parts that just glow.

A book is like the ocean,
Can be hard to get through,
Can be tough,
When you've just had enough,
With the lies and the truth.

A book is like a time traveller,
One day, you're here,
Or in the future,
Feeling like a winner,
Having read William Shakespeare.

A book is an adventure,
Here, there, everywhere,
A treat which is oh so rare,
All in this text,
I wonder what's next?

Neasa Hughes (12)
Sandymoor Ormiston Academy, Sandymoor

Lemons And Watermelons

Lemons and watermelons,
What a weird combination,
I'm hearing these phrases all over the nation,
Lemons are sour,
Watermelons have a weird texture,
Lemons are better than watermelons,
Watermelons are better than lemons,
How could we settle this debate?
But not argue with a mate,
Lemons and watermelons both share their juiciness,
Watermelons are easy to eat and can be cut into different sizes and shapes,
Lemons are harder to eat but have any amazing sour flavour,
But lemons do create a sour face,
So let's settle this debate,
Lemons or watermelons?

Jenson Tildsley (12)
Sandymoor Ormiston Academy, Sandymoor

Pollution

Pollution is a bad thing,
It hurts our environment,
It won't stop getting worse,
It is like a disease we can't help,
People try and help,
It is not enough though,
Pick up your rubbish,
Try to help,
Pollution is a bad thing,
It hurts our environment,
It won't stop getting worse,
It is like a disease we can't help,
It's okay to be sad,
It's okay to be mad,
Help the world,
Save your planet,
Pollution is a bad thing,
It hurts our environment,
It won't stop getting worse,
Like a disease we can't help.

Holly Talbot (12)
Sandymoor Ormiston Academy, Sandymoor

The Lighthouse

The lighthouse watching over the sea,
Waiting for her children to come back home,
Back to the bay,
Then out they go again, away.
Their mother weeps as she circles,
Waiting for her dear children to come home,
Some stay by their mother,
And some are lost at sea.
One day, the bay was happy,
But as night came,
Horror struck for the mother and her children,
The earth shook and a terrible storm rolled in.
Houses fell and the poor children floated out to sea,
Their poor mother wept once more before she fell.
From that day on, the children stayed nearby.

Anastasia Procek (12)
Sandymoor Ormiston Academy, Sandymoor

My Favourite Place Is Earth

My favourite place is Earth,
There's no better in this universe,
But negative change needs to be prevented,
Our Earth must be protected.

My favourite place is Earth,
But these changes are for the worst,
And soon there may be nothing left,
But we can save it if we all try our best.

My favourite place is Earth,
But our planet is starting to hurt,
So let's all do our part,
Before this planet falls apart.

My favourite place is Earth,
So let's stop the hurt,
Because if we all work together,
Our Earth will be better.

Calvin Roberts (11)
Sandymoor Ormiston Academy, Sandymoor

Don't Give Up

If you give up, you'll never achieve your dreams,
You can lurk together as a team,
If you give up, you won't feel proud of yourself,
Don't listen to people trying to pull you down.

You may say it'll tire you out,
But it will be worth it, without a doubt,
Just ask your parents to support you,
No matter what you choose to do.

I'm writing this poem to tell you:
Never give up on what you want to achieve,
Don't let the bad people tell you you'll never get there,
Because I know you can, if you put your mind to it.

Finlay Pitcher (12)
Sandymoor Ormiston Academy, Sandymoor

Vanish Poverty

S upermarkets are selling food, it's happening really fast,
T o us, that's normal, buy, eat, repeat,
O thers struggle financially,
P arents send their kids to bed hungry,

P reparing themselves for small meals,
O ur responsibility is to help those need,
V anish poverty and donate to the food bank,
E very single food donation counts,
R ethink, just throwing out stuff you don't like,
T ake it to those people who need it most,
Y ou can make a difference!

Holly Tasker (12)
Sandymoor Ormiston Academy, Sandymoor

Devices Are Really Useful

Devices are really useful,
Almost all the world are using them,
They can be used for interacting with people around the world,
Devices are really useful,
You can research about countries without having to visit them,
It would be so useful and easy to use them,
You can learn and educate yourself with them,
Devices are so useful,
All devices are used, day and night,
It might hurt your brain if you use them a lot,
Or it may damage your eyes if you use them too,
But still, devices are useful, and we use them day and night.

Mouamen Ashour (12)
Sandymoor Ormiston Academy, Sandymoor

Never Waste Food

Waste your food, never do it,
More starving people, bit by bit,
Eat it up, everything,
So every day, you can spring,

If you put food in the bin,
You will commit a sin,
Only put on your plate the right amount,
Don't put too much that it is hard to count,

Eat with your friends or family,
And enjoy it happily,
Say a prayer,
And eat with care,

Waste your food, never do it,
More starving people, bit by bit,
Now that you have learnt your lesson,
We should see such a progression.

Mia O'Mahoney (13)
Sandymoor Ormiston Academy, Sandymoor

Mushrooms

Mushrooms are vile,
They smell worse than my washing pile,
They taste like funky socks,
And smell like unwashed locks,
Mushrooms feel like slimy snails,
When I eat them, I go pale,
I have to hold my nose,
Tastes like they've been growing between my toes,
I would rather eat a cow pat,
Or a leather hat,
Mushrooms taste stranger than that,
If I ate enough, they could knock me out,
So infuriatingly bad, they make me want to shout,
Mushrooms taste so funny,
To eat one, you would have to pay me money.

Charly Fuller (12)
Sandymoor Ormiston Academy, Sandymoor

Swimming Is King!

Swimming is king!
Who doesn't like it?
It gives you exercise,
And peace of mind.

Swimming is king!
Who doesn't like it?
You only need to splash
To get on track.

Swimming is king!
Who doesn't like it?
Enjoy gentle waves
For days after days.

Swimming is king!
Who doesn't like it?
Competitiveness to its peak,
Win, unless you're weak.

Swimming is dangerous,
Why should you like it?
What it brings
Outweighs those things.

Oliver Baskeyfield (12)
Sandymoor Ormiston Academy, Sandymoor

Rugby

Rugby is the best sport,
You can't tell me differently,
All of the sports I have tried,
Rugby is the best sport,
You might say football all the way,
And I must say okay,
I love rugby more,
And that will never change,
However, I like football too, but not as much,
I love rugby because of the attitude,
And the passing play and the attacking play of the players,
I play because it makes me happy for the day,
At the end of the day,
Rugby is the best sport to play.

Hari Owen (11)
Sandymoor Ormiston Academy, Sandymoor

Onion Bhajis

Onion bhajis are a gift from heaven,
Not slimy, not dry, just perfect all the time,
Not too soft, not too hard.

Onion bhajis fit just fine,
Not too sweet like sugar, not too salty like the sea,
They have the taste of a god.

Onion bhajis overpower all food,
Other food can just get booed,
They're just super flavourful, dude.

Onion bhajis will always be on top,
No matter what,
So head down to your nearest food shop,
And get as many as you want.

Jack Rogers (12)
Sandymoor Ormiston Academy, Sandymoor

Summer Breeze

The world has come alive,
All the bees are coming out of their hives,
All I hear are the birds,
And the way they speak their private words,
The Earth is rising,
All of its beauty is surprising,

Others might say birds are pests,
But no, they are the best!
They will always bring
Something good to sing,

All the families are shouting,
They will never be doubting,
Remember to fasten your seatbelt,
Because all the best is about to be dealt.

Jeremiasz Krawczyk (12)
Sandymoor Ormiston Academy, Sandymoor

Football

Football is always fun,
Since you can always run,
Football will boost your mood,
As well as make you cool.

Football is all about passing,
It is rough with grabbing,
Kick the ball with your boot,
Because the crowd yell, "Shoot!"

Football sometimes gets you down,
End the game with a frown,
Your team will sometimes lose,
The crowd will sometimes boo.

Your team might win titles,
To others, looking quite frightful.

Ben Brizell (13)
Sandymoor Ormiston Academy, Sandymoor

The Sea Is Beautiful

The sea is beautiful,
The planets will wriggle every night,
The creatures of the sea have beauty,
Under what you can't see, there is life.

The sea is beautiful,
As you don't know when it stops,
The sea is endless, it goes for life,
It is free, you cannot control the sea.

The sea is beautiful,
It is calm,
The look of waves will hypnotise you,
So will the sound of the sea.

The sea is beautiful,
Have a look.

Nikola Lewandowska (13)
Sandymoor Ormiston Academy, Sandymoor

Carrot Cake Is A Great Cake

Carrot cake is a great cake,
It has lots of flavour,
You can have it a lot,
But you might be sick,
Carrot cake is a great cake.

You think it doesn't work together,
But you have not tried,
It can be bad the first time,
But you might like it the next,
Carrot cake is a great cake.

Some people like it, some don't,
It has good spices,
With cream on top,
There's nothing to hate,
Carrot cake is a great cake.

Ellie Costigan (13)
Sandymoor Ormiston Academy, Sandymoor

The Sky

I admire the sky more than anyone,
I think it would be a disaster if there was none,
Even if it goes grey,
It shines at the end of the day,

Even when it's day,
It may turn grey,
Even when it's night,
It's still a little bit bright,

I love the sky, head to toe,
Especially when there is a little rainbow,
I think the sky would weigh a ton,
I admire the sky more than anyone.

Luke Keenan (12)
Sandymoor Ormiston Academy, Sandymoor

We Will Fight!

People say we can't put a stop
To the Earth's plot,
The plot of over-heating,
It's going to be beating
The human race, we'll soon be gone,
And we will be done,
But no!
I will go,
And I will fight
For our future rights,
And I don't want you
To be blue,
So come fasten your seatbelt
For the ride of your life,
And let's put a stop
To the Earth's plot.

Kristofer Klepets (11)
Sandymoor Ormiston Academy, Sandymoor

Football Is The Best

Football is the best,
Kick a ball,
Header a ball,
Football is the best.

Football is the best,
You can't convince me otherwise,
Not telling any lies,
Football is the best.

Football is the best,
Some people hate it,
Some people adore it,
Football is the best.

Football is the best,
Rashford is the king,
He's better than Mings,
Football is the best.

Daniel Jones (12)
Sandymoor Ormiston Academy, Sandymoor

Mental Health Is Important!

Mental health is important,
It is a real thing,
You may think it is fake,
But it really is a struggle!
People you know
May be sat at home,
And sat worrying about the unknown,
With bad mental health,
You will struggle with yourself,
You view life as a game,
And feel you fail to reach your aim,
Which ends in a bad situation,
But this is not it all,
This is mental health!

Jack James (12)
Sandymoor Ormiston Academy, Sandymoor

Liverpool

L oud Champion's League nights,
I njured players occur a lot,
V an Dijk is our trusted centre half,
E vertonians can't compare to us Reds,
R ed is our iconic colour,
P aul Scholes is not on Gerrard's level,
O ur leader, the beloved Jürgen Klopp,
O bviously, we are the best team in England,
L ively days at Anfield Stadium.

Harry Simpson (12)
Sandymoor Ormiston Academy, Sandymoor

KFC, The Best In The World

KFC is so good, no matter the day,
It couldn't be bad, whatever you say,
I could eat it in no time,
And it would only cost a dime.

I would eat it while she's teaching,
The menu, I would eat everything,
The chicken is so tender,
There is also a KFC in Chester.

KFC is so heavenly,
I would eat it happily,
And I would love it,
Every single bit.

Jack Metcalfe (13)
Sandymoor Ormiston Academy, Sandymoor

Family And Friends

My family and friends are my favourite,
I love them to death and that's a promise,
They include me everywhere they go,

My family and friends are my favourite,
They make me laugh and cheer me up,
They solve my problems and keep me safe,

My family and friends are my favourite,
They spoil me rotten and are very generous,
We all need family and friends.

Bethany Dimelow (13)
Sandymoor Ormiston Academy, Sandymoor

Have Self-Belief

Never stop believing in yourself,
Because you can do anything in life,
As long as you put your mind to it.

Your friends and family will support you,
No matter what,
And if anyone tells you what to do in life,
Just say, no!

You are your own person,
You do what you want in life,
As long as it makes you happy,
Never stop believing in yourself.

Maya Hanson (12)
Sandymoor Ormiston Academy, Sandymoor

Knife Crime

Knife crime is terrible,
You should never do it,
But if you do it, you will always regret it,
You might think it's good for revenge,
But it is never,
You will ruin your life,
And others',
Knife crime is terrible,
You will be arrested,
And be hated,
You will always feel sorry
For what you have done,
Knife crime is terrible.

Harry Huby (13)
Sandymoor Ormiston Academy, Sandymoor

Drugs Are Wrong

Drugs are wrong,
You should never do them,
It costs money,
And if you do it,
You might overdose,
If you're addicted,
You can't stop,
If you do drugs,
You might find yourself
Behind bars for some time,
Some people think it's cool
And fun,
But really,
It's poisonous and dangerous,
Don't do drugs!

Finlay Mason (12)
Sandymoor Ormiston Academy, Sandymoor

The World Of Football

F un to watch and play,
O n the TV every day, even Saturday,
O verall amazing sport,
T he players use every skill they've been taught,
B allers on the move,
A nd usually celebrate with a groove,
L et's all celebrate,
L oving football for me is not a debate.

Dylan Faragher (11)
Sandymoor Ormiston Academy, Sandymoor

The World Of Football

F un to watch and play,
O n the TV every Saturday,
O verall amazing sport,
T he players dive when they've been onslaught,
B allers on a move,
A nd they even celebrate with a groove,
L et's all celebrate,
L oving football for me is no debate.

Joe Fahimi (12)
Sandymoor Ormiston Academy, Sandymoor

Guns Away

Ban guns, everything is cool,
Just ban guns, that is all.

Giving teachers guns - no problem at all!
That is not solving problems,
Not at all,
Just ban guns, that is all!

If guns go away, hip, hip hooray!
I wish it were just today,
Guns away, just please, maybe today!

Josh Totten (12)
Sandymoor Ormiston Academy, Sandymoor

Knife Crime: I Hate Knife Crime

Knife crime should be stopped,
It is so deceitful,
It is more common than a train being delayed,
You may not think this,
But people lose lives 'cause of this,
Just stop,
You think you are all hard,
Because you carry a knife,
When you're not,
So stop knife crime.

Corey Birch-McClure (12)
Sandymoor Ormiston Academy, Sandymoor

All Football

F un to play with mates,
O r even your relatives,
O verall the best,
T hey even get a test,
B rilliant game to play,
A ll the way until the end of the day,
L ots of people praying when there is a penalty,
L ots of people playing.

Liam O'Connell (12)
Sandymoor Ormiston Academy, Sandymoor

Rain

Rain, rain, pouring down,
You make me happy, others frown,
You rap against my windowpane,
I hear the wind blow again,
Others may disagree, as you create floods,
However, I will let down my hood!
You brighten my day,
What else to say?
Except for, rain, I hope you stay!

Pippa Smith-Cole (12)
Sandymoor Ormiston Academy, Sandymoor

Fantastic Football

F ierce tackles,
O nly 90 minutes,
O verall amazing sport,
T eams across the world,
B eautiful game,
A mazing fanbases,
L oud crowds,
L ove and passion for everyone.

Harrison Shingler (12)
Sandymoor Ormiston Academy, Sandymoor

Evolution

With a little scribble in my little hand, I go show my mother,
"Amazing drawing, honey, you're improving!"
With that little scribble, I go show my brother,
"Why are her arms and legs sticks?" is his reply,
"Oh, shut up! No one cares anyway," I shout back,
He says, "Mum always says it's not good to lie."

With a bigger drawing in my bigger hand, I go to show my mother,
"Oh, that's nice, you've definitely improved, dear."
With that little drawing, I go to show my brother,
"Nice, but the proportions are off," he replies,
"Hey! I tried really hard," I say back,
He says, "You just asked for my opinion, so yeah, bye."

I hope to have amazing pieces of artwork,
Large and beautiful with a special meaning,
Incredibly stunning, it would make heads jerk,
Despite the fact it would have taken long,
And that it may have taken many days,
It would be the result of long years of hard work.

Rithika Raj (11)
St Pius X Catholic High School, Wath Upon Dearne

Build A Better World

You can twiddle your thumbs like Nero and Rome,
And poison your planet, your haven, your home,
Your people are sheep, forever will they follow,
As you lead them unknowingly into the darkness of tomorrow...

Our world stands on edge, ready to fall or soar,
To let fly the doves of peace, or let ballistic missiles roar,
These inevitable results of years of turmoil,
Conflicts over land, power, and oil.

Fingers clutch the keys and the switch,
Eager to push, to pull, like an itch,
Which will you choose, riches or war?
Are you satisfied with little or craving for more?

For it's ours not to reason why,
Ours not to crouch or cry,
Ours not to scream or sigh,
Ours but to do and to die.

Ours not to cheat and lie,
Ours not to faint or fly,
Ours not to shout or snivel under the everlasting fury of death's remorseless eye,
Ours but to do and to die.

So ignore our every word, our every little plea,
And set forth your fleets to fight for our seas,
Send your missiles flying, not just sticks and stones,
Bombs that destroy families, nations, homes.

But just think,
Think of your family, your sweet little daughter,
As you guide them blindly like a lamb to the slaughter,
Think of your parents, your poor little son,
With no place to hide, to flee or run,
You could save their fruitful, joyful laughter,
Or become the hangman's hands of this global disaster...

However you want to take it, poem, sonnet, song,
Appreciate the costs of right and wrong,
We're all a brother, a mother, a father, a son,
Yet we look at each other down the barrel of a gun.

War brings no benefit, nothing but death,
Pain and suffering, 'til the last strained breath,
So let us cast out these villains of the past,
And build a better world, for our children, to last...

Joshua Griffiths (13)
St Pius X Catholic High School, Wath Upon Dearne

Life

"Mother, don't leave me!"
We all shout whenever afraid,
Hoping life will go on forever,
Knowing what is ahead, we fear,
We fear and fear until that fear engulfs us,
Nothing disappears, the thought, the memory,
The feeling of their presence lingers behind,
And pulls you down like a weight,
Death gives us sleep, eternal youth and immortality,
Death is described differently all around,
Death, the way to return to the light, you are found,
I did not love them for the feeling or title,
I fell in love with them because they cared for me,
I peacefully watched them sleep,
Now from their grave, I weep,
Some people mourn, some people are torn,
Some are buried, some are burned,
It doesn't matter, it's all a part of life,
Maybe in another life, it's a cruel life,
No matter what I do, everything brings me back to life,
"Don't leave me, Mother!"
I cried that day my mother crossed the road,
No one to hold her back,
As her limbs became numb and her vision was impaired,
She slipped away, silently,

I became unaware of my surroundings, I screamed,
I screamed until something inside my throat broke,
My mother crossed the road, now it's all grey,
My mother crossed the road, it's all my fault,
I can't cry, nor scream, just accept it,
As I sit above her grave,
We will walk into darkness, hoping for the light,
That simply is life.

Elodia Stanley (11)
St Pius X Catholic High School, Wath Upon Dearne

Long Live Ukraine

Rat-tat-tat,
The sound of guns fills the air,
My family has fled,
I don't sleep in a bed,
Because of this war,
My house has no front door,
I have a gun in my hands,
And it's not just a war between two bands,
No, this is more,
I am fighting this war
For my country to live forever more.

Kyiv shall not be taken,
Nor will my life be taken,
For the field of wheat with blue skies,
My country's flag will never fade,
I will battle 'til the end of time,
Just to make sure that the winner of this war will be mine.

Behind the lines,
I am not just a man,
I am a father,
I am a son,
I am a brother,
But yet I only see my family,
Only twice a month,

I have to hope my phone isn't broken,
As it is my only form of communication.

But here I am more,
Much, much more,
I am a soldier,
I am an officer,
I am a leader,
Even my friend, Ivan,
And my brother, Davyd,
Even my long-time rival, Igor,
We are united as one,
I stand over them, waiting for the signal,
Charge!

I dodge the bullets as I run
Into the enemy's trench,
Many have fallen, they will be avenged,
Their families will want revenge
For these war crimes,
That are yet to end.

No, this is not just a war between two bands,
No, this is more,
I am fighting for my country
To live forever more.

Emilia Cichy (13)
St Pius X Catholic High School, Wath Upon Dearne

Healing

I finally found the one,
He treats me how he should,
Now he is gone,
But he loved me how he should.

I loved him,
I loved when he'd throw me out of bed,
I loved when he'd hit me,
I loved when he'd shout at me,
I loved when he'd call me names,
I loved walking out the room, bleeding from his wrath.

I loved him,
It was true love, right?
Now it's all over,
He was an idiot,
But he was my idiot.

Some of my friends have healed after a day,
Or maybe a week,
Some, a year,
Although I know how to heal,
I can heal, just not from this,
It has left a mark,
Now I'm sitting in the dark,
A bite on my shoulder,
He is a petrifying shark.

I loved him,
He was nice, right?
I cried and cried, he slammed the door,
I don't know what to feel anymore,
I want to go home,
He was my home,
My home is on fire,
Just like my heart,
My home is all angry,
My life has become dark.

We are all stars to disappear or die,
I should learn to look at an empty sky,
And feel it's subliminal,
Though through time, it will take a little.

Elodia Stanley (11)
St Pius X Catholic High School, Wath Upon Dearne

I'd Pick You

If we were in a field full of flowers, I'd pick you,
You don't believe me,
Or if you do, you think I should pick somebody else,
Someone prettier, someone kinder,
Because anyone will be better than you,
Well, that's just not true.

You've always failed to see your true worth,
Others see you as sunshine, a rainbow,
But you see yourself as a tornado, a hurricane,
Then you should consider me the storm chaser,
A bit of rain and wind can't hurt, right?

I'll pick you in the darkest of dark moments,
And in your finest hours,
I'll take you if nobody else will,
And if you ever find someone you love more,
More prepared for your storms,
I'll let you go.

Just know,
I'll always be here with my umbrella and raincoat to do it over again,
Ten thousand times more, because
I'd pick you.

Danielle Lukey (15)
St Pius X Catholic High School, Wath Upon Dearne

I Am Yorkshire

From the seams of Yorkshire, I was born,
Waking up without a yawn,
Go-karting and Cannon Hall farm,
And visiting Whitby to feel calm.

I am a Yorkshire boy, big and strong,
But I still love my mum,
I may be a little dumb,
Still, I love some Yorkshire puds in my tum'.

This is Yorkshire, full of fields of green,
Yorkshire moors would've been
The worst place you've ever seen,
If Boris had touched this perfect place of the bean.

I've been on a car ride,
I'm surprised I haven't died,
I have got myself tied
In bad situations where I almost cried.

This is Yorkshire, perfect as can be,
Greatly beautiful and my home definitely,
I am Yorkshire, this is me,
I was born and hope to die in the beautiful land of Yorkshire.

Christopher Reading
St Pius X Catholic High School, Wath Upon Dearne

Yorkshire Paradise

Sunshine shining, seagulls chirping,
What a lovely day,
My neighbour, a young pal,
Walking with his Yorkshire terrier
On a lovely walk to Yorkshire Wildlife Park.

I love my Sunday dinners in summer,
When it's sunny, with my mates,
Eating the most magnificent Yorkshire puddings,
Looking like lovely crowns with delicious gravy!

While in the garden,
A white Yorkshire rose blooms in my flower pot,
Shining across the garden,
Glowing like the sunshine in the sky,
Dogs are barking and playing in fields,
Kids playing football outside,
Playing with friends and being kind to each other,
What a lovely day.

I go to sleep in bed,
And the sun is going down,
It's goodnight for me,
Now I have to say goodbye!

Maja Wegrzyn (11)
St Pius X Catholic High School, Wath Upon Dearne

My Yorkshire Culture

As I ride my bike to the Wildlife Park,
The only place in England that has polar bears,
I feel the Yorkshire wind crash into my face,
As I hear the Wednesday fans shouting and singing,
This is Yorkshire!

When I ride past Avago Cart,
I hear the laughing of the children,
And see their mum's drinking Yorkshire tea,
While eating their Sunday dinner, especially with Yorkshire puddings,
This is Yorkshire!

Then I ride past the most beautiful place, Conisbrough Castle,
I think of all the history that has happened in England,
Especially Yorkshire,
This is Yorkshire!

Then there is the pet shop,
With the cutest pets,
I see the Yorkshire terrier,
That is when I get off my bike,
Because this is Yorkshire!

Ebony Bull (11)
St Pius X Catholic High School, Wath Upon Dearne

My Dream

I leap across the jelly lake,
Across large cakes, freshly baked,
The candy cane trees,
And gumdrop bees,
The smell of chocolate pleases me,
Marshmallows like little beds,
For the Haribo hippos to rest their heads,
The candyfloss clouds, up in the sky,
Which fairies touch when they fly,
The feeling of this magical place,
Gives me a feeling like no other place,
The lovely lemon-scented air,
The only rule is you have to share,
The gummy bears are a playful bunch,
A crunchy bar is their favourite lunch,
But suddenly, this place is no more,
I hear the sound of my clock 'roar',
It's seven o'clock and I stare into space,
Waiting for night so I can zoom back into my place.

Isabelle Leary (13)
St Pius X Catholic High School, Wath Upon Dearne

Daisy

Roses are red,
Violets are blue,
Every second of class,
I think of you,

I love when I hug you,
And you do too,
Even when everyone is watching,
I'll say, "I love you!"

At break and lunch,
My fave part of the day,
We hang out,
And I say, "Hooray!"

If I got a pound every time I thought of you,
I would have £1,
Because you never leave my mind,
Because you're mine,

Now that I have found you,
My life is complete,
Because no one can compete with you,
Daisy,

I'm so glad your mine,
So thank you,
For being my valentine.

Joe Ellis (11)
St Pius X Catholic High School, Wath Upon Dearne

England's Best League

P assion in players' hearts,
R etired players in the stands,
E ventually clashed lands become rivals,
M any players could even just play for the price of a trifle,
I n a few matches, you'd be memorised,
E very team has an iconic moment,
R ooney was one of United's best,

L ost future legends add weight on their chest,
E veryone can play in this league, even from afar,
A nyone who plays football can be a star,
G ive young players time,
U nderstand how rare they can be,
E very player has passion, but most people say it's just a game!

Max Gumienny (12)
St Pius X Catholic High School, Wath Upon Dearne

My Yorkshire Culture

As the rain hits the window,
I'm sitting with some good old
warm Yorkshire tea
and a nice beautiful
Sunday dinner,
with lots of Yorkshire puddings.
This is Yorkshire!

After I finish,
I go to the Yorkshire Wildlife
on my bike,
with the fresh breezy air
hitting my face,
seeing the children running around,
getting amused,
seeing all the animals.
This is Yorkshire!

Returning home from a great day
at the Yorkshire Wildlife,
to see my Yorkshire terrier,
Bob, sat down,
waiting for a good old nag.
This is my Yorkshire!

Alexi Hague (12)
St Pius X Catholic High School, Wath Upon Dearne

The Greatest Save

One-on-one, my heart is pounding,
All the fans are shouting and chanting,

Standing there is the penalty shooter,
If only that foul was a little bit further,

He takes a couple steps back, getting ready,
There I stand, looking steady,

He runs to the ball and kicks top-left,
There I am, staring at the ball mid-dive,

Having no hope of saving it,
I stretch my arm a tiny bit more,
And there it is,

The greatest save of history,
My fingers barely touched the ball,
But it will do,
No goal!

Patrik Krajci (13)
St Pius X Catholic High School, Wath Upon Dearne

This Is Yorkshire Life!

I'm a full Yorkshire lad, born and bred,
I'm a tad thick in 'ed,
I love Yorkshire tea lying in bed,
Yorkshire life is the best!

Walk down to the pub for a drink and some grub,
Go home for a nap and nip down to the local tap,
To get a pint with my mates,
We're in a state,
Yorkshire life is the best!

Have a Sunday dinner,
And wonder why I'm getting no thinner,
Get a loan and nip to the Dome,
Yorkshire life is the best!

Check out the local match,
Yorkshire life is the best!

Jack Wigley (12)
St Pius X Catholic High School, Wath Upon Dearne

This Is Yorkshire!

This is Yorkshire!
We have many activities,
From dance to drinking tea,
Or you could go shopping
With your mates at Meadowhall,
Or go for a trip to Cannon Hall,
This is Yorkshire!
We have our fishing bait,
And our lovely accent, mate,
Go fishing at the moors,
And have the bait brought to your door,
While looking at Yorkshire walls,
This is Yorkshire!
Come here to play,
Just for the day,
Or come to stay,
For a beer at the pub,
Or just a lunch,
Because this is Yorkshire!

Zack Foster (11)
St Pius X Catholic High School, Wath Upon Dearne

My Yorkshire Culture Poem

Oi, do you want a cuppa tea?
Or a bottle of water?
Or else you'll just get fatter,
This is Yorkshire.

Join me for a barbie,
Are you just being naughty?
This is Yorkshire.

Do you want a Sunday dinner
With Yorkshire puddings?
Are you just upsetting your bloomin' tummy?
This is Yorkshire.

If you want a treat,
How about you have one of Yorkshire's mixed sweets?
This is Yorkshire.

I love Yorkshire to the full,
Just give it a little pull.

Harvey Roy Dennis Penrose (12)
St Pius X Catholic High School, Wath Upon Dearne

Football Dreams

She wakes up every day, thinking of the great game,
Football is its great name.

Girls can't play football is what they say,
But have they ever seen her play?

To make it pro is her dream,
Seeing all the floodlights beam.

The crowd chanting her name,
Will she be able to bring herself fame?

She worked hard to get here,
Just to hear the fans cheer.

Football dreams are to remember,
I guess we will find out at her trial in September.

Safiya Kettlewell (13)
St Pius X Catholic High School, Wath Upon Dearne

This Is My Yorkshire!

Drinking a cup of tea,
Or I'm in the pub with my friends and me,
Watching Barnsley lose again,
They just play like ordinary men,
Trying to get away, so I'm travelling to Xscape,
Going down and up those slopes does keep me in shape!
I went to the bank to get a loan,
So I can go to Barnsley Metrodome,
Wait! My Yorkshire terrier is at home,
All those Pukka pies sure to crumble,
I'm coming back from the match listening to Talksport,
praise or grumble.

Isaac Law (12)
St Pius X Catholic High School, Wath Upon Dearne

The Seaside Chip Robbers

When you're at the seaside, be warned,
The seaside chip robbers are everywhere,
Some are even in the air,
Don't be fooled, don't be tricked,
The seaside chip robbers will nick your chips,
They fly and twirl and then they chant,
That's the chip robber dance,
They dive down from the air
Like they don't care,
Some are in formation like army planes,
And some are on the ground like soldiers,
Their mission is to go on a feeding frenzy.

Charlie Tracy-Taylor (12)
St Pius X Catholic High School, Wath Upon Dearne

My Culture Poem

From the Vikings, I was born,
Now Yorkshire is my home!
All the lads walk down to the pub,
"Na then young'un, hows the father doin'?"
Listening to TalkSport on our way from the football,
As our loveable tykes win once again,
As a Yorkshire brew is supped like usual,
As me and my mates mess about
On the Sunday league pitches,
Pretending to be Sergio Ramos,
Tackling each other,
This is Yorkshire,
And this is my home!

Elliott Hanson (11)
St Pius X Catholic High School, Wath Upon Dearne

Yorkshire

Y orkshire puddings are what I like to eat,
O ur beautiful sands of Scarborough on my feet,
R ain is a usual thing in Yorkshire,
K icking a ball through a muddy field,
S haring my chips at the seaside with friends,
H aving scored a goal at a football match,
I cy roads in the winter,
R oast dinners with family on Sundays,
E very day in Yorkshire is always a fun day.

Prada Bates (11)
St Pius X Catholic High School, Wath Upon Dearne

This Is Yorkshire!

I woke up and put on my school top,
I go on my phone and check the mop,
I take my pet to the Yorkshire vet,
While fishermen go out to sea,
I ask the bank for a loan,
I go to Doncaster Dome,
This is Yorkshire!
I go back home for breakfast in bed,
Sausage, beans, bacon, and eggs,
Craftsmen making lead pains my head,
Go to the local bakery while they're freshly making bread,
This is Yorkshire!

Dillon Kitchen (11)
St Pius X Catholic High School, Wath Upon Dearne

Seaside Fair

I fly across a living tree,
With birds that fly alongside me,
Then I see a jelly lake,
It must have been a jelly fake,
The lovely scented air,
Then you arrive at a seaside fair,
The rides, the candyfloss, the sweet doughnuts,
The donkeys, the golden sand,
All jump into my waiting hands,
I run along the sandy beach,
The cold grey sea is within my reach.

Harriet Allen (13)
St Pius X Catholic High School, Wath Upon Dearne

My Yorkshire Poem

Sunday morning, I ride my bike down the Yorkshire hills,
And look at the mills,
Go-kart racing with my mates,
On my way home, I nip to the shop,
And buy a bottle of pop,
Fishy and chippies for tea,
Looking out of the window,
Seeing Yorkshire men in flat caps,
With a can of beer and a Yorkshire terrier by their side,
This is a true Yorkshire day!

Lily Towlerton (12)
St Pius X Catholic High School, Wath Upon Dearne

My Yorkshire Poem

Scarborough is like heaven when you're with a dog,
Unless you're with your sister - "Mia, I swear to God!"
The memories of Yorkshire Wildlife Park,
Eating a lolly, walking home in the dark.
The accents, though hard to understand,
Are a part of our land.
Yes, the rain is a pain,
But this is our home,
This is Yorkshire.

Ava Poole (11)
St Pius X Catholic High School, Wath Upon Dearne

The Yorkshire Girl

A hungry Yorkshire girl,
Dancing in a lovely twirl,
Singing a song that makes her hair curl,
After dinner, a cup of tea is nice,
And with her dinner, she had boiled rice,
But that led out the starving mice,
Instead, she drove to Whitby,
To taste the fish and chips,
And stayed in a hotel
To have a pleasant sleep.

Louisa Nayar (11)
St Pius X Catholic High School, Wath Upon Dearne

My Culture Poem

Kebabs at the chippy,
Ice cream, Mr Whippy,
At the park 'til dark,
'Cause my head feelin' dizzy,
Cultural poem's got me weak,
Like playing hide-and-seek,
'Cause I'm at my highest peak,
Yes, this is Yorkshire!
Can you breathe it in?
Yes, this is Yorkshire!
Now time for my departure.

Jaiden Hill (11)
St Pius X Catholic High School, Wath Upon Dearne

Born In Yorkshire

I was born in Yorkshire,
Sippin' some tea,
While on my grandma's knee,
Going to Yorkshire Wildlife Park,
Trying to spot a scary shark,
Go to Meadowhall,
Oops, I ran into a Yorkshire Dales stone wall,
Walked outside and got a startle,
Gasp! They are knocking down Conisbrough Castle!

Isaac Garrett (11)
St Pius X Catholic High School, Wath Upon Dearne

My Home

All the way from home, Ukraine,
To Yorkshire, cold, grey and different,
I started school and made good friends,
But it's not my Ukraine,
Yorkshire tea is nice, it's true,
But for my Ukraine, I am ready to give my life,
I love this grey Yorkshire,
But it's not my sunny home.

Yuliia Rohach (11)
St Pius X Catholic High School, Wath Upon Dearne

I Think I'm In A Dream

Sometimes, I think I'm in a dream,
And most things I see aren't what they seem,
Sometimes, I think I'm in a dream,
Watching everything closely as though through a screen,
Sometimes, I think I'm in a dream,
Until I hear the horrible school bell scream.

Julia Moyo (13)
St Pius X Catholic High School, Wath Upon Dearne

The Hidden Disease

Racism is a disease
And don't try to disagree
Because whether you're Portuguese
Or speak Cantonese
Or called Abdul-Aziz
Or have skin the colour of cream
You know that it hasn't yet ceased

Everywhere
Symptoms of racism float in the air
Until one doesn't care
And breathes in the virus and becomes unfair

We hear the term 'racism' in the news
And how people's pride forces them to violently abuse
And I'm so confused
Why does another identity allow you to accuse
And both physically and mentally bruise
Another person who is different from you?

Racism has become a norm
That will slowly form
A terrible storm
That will force humanity to be torn

Who remembers Hitler's demonisation?
Killing all the Jews was his operation
Some were able to take part in the evacuation
Palestine is the next location
Apartheid is their situation
Where every day people suffer starvation
They are only aided by donations
Who will come to their salvation
Like how South Africa went through a transformation
When Nelson Mandela became their illumination
Who will rebuild Palestine's foundations

Martin Luther King said that he had a dream
But that dream is becoming worse and going off-stream
Why does the regime
Do nothing but daydream
When they hear innocent screams
It's always the same theme

Who remembers George Floyd?
He was killed because the police were annoyed
And then we think of Stephen Lawrence
Murdered by boys who were filled with abhorrence
Bukayo Saka missed a penalty
He was damaged mentally
And picked on especially
Because of his identity

Sadly that is how we live
Always in the negative
Like come on, you gotta be better representatives

To the next generations
That will be your cruel imitations
I'm trying to tell you that we are all the same creation
But to my frustration
Your admiration
Strengthens this ignorant worldwide organisation
Watch out, because my aspiration
And determination
Will become the deflation
To this disgraceful association

Our hearts are the centre of our body frames
Pumping blood that is all the same
Even though we have unique names
Don't follow your evil flame
It will lead you astray
That's all I'm trying to convey.

Ibrahim Khalid (11)
Vyners School, Ickenham

Sacrifices

S evere losses, casualties, wounds, and many more problems to report to our general in this damned trench,
A merican P-51s soaring across the horizon into German territory to drop devastating loads on the capital,
C entral slaughterhouses were there, places where they tortured, interrogated, and murdered those innocent civilians,
R inging in my ears from those grenades which pushed the mud, heavy with the smell of blood,
I mmense sacrifices were made for our beloved king, most of the time in vain,
F ormer kind mates have changed to savage dogs, bursting their machine guns at anyone in sight,
I solated survivors from the lucy Air Force pilots, stranded in the middle of nowhere, usually captured by the Axis forces,
C an I not afford a single moment to see any kindness, love, or time for others?
E motions hit you much harder than they did in ol' London, a single friend you only know for a few days smashed you in the heart like a missile,
S o the war was a hard time for us British, but nobody can feel like I did when I felt that bomb, it hurt, it hurt more than anything else, it was the end.

Parth Joshi (12)
Vyners School, Ickenham

Romantic Roulette

That feeling of having someone to hold close,
Whenever, wherever, however you need it,
Like an eternal pinky promise
To stay by someone's side,
Out of the pure want to.
Most people yearn endlessly for it,
Welcome it with open arms,
And hold onto it for as long as they can.

But I?
I never gave it that chance.

Oftentimes, cats will keep their bellies protected,
Only show it to those they deeply trust,
After all, it's the most vulnerable part of their body,
I suppose that was true for me.

I was always a tough kid growing up,
My skin grew thicker with every insult thrown at my body.
But the only place where people could truly help me,
Or hurt me, was my heart.

I could never welcome love with open arms,
It always felt like some sick joke
That everyone was in on,

Except me.

Like everyone looking at you,
Snickering when you come up in conversation.

People like me learn to hide,
Create a facade,
So they can never be hurt again,
But the guise of comedy
Is a powerful teacher.
It shows you just how little you really know yourself,
How you can end up making yourself believe that
Everything is fine.
It's like hiding in plain sight,
For a good offence is simply
A variation of defence.

You end up believing
That this facade serves you,
When really all it does
Is leaves you unprepared.
For, one day, like a subtle yet rushing gale,
So blustering, your heart forgets how to work,
For a moment, that same armoured heart
Will let its guard down.

Love will hail toward you,
Bringing confusion in its stead,
Leaving you pondering for weeks,
Consuming your hours,
Strumming a dance of death

On your heartstrings,
To the point where you grow insatiable,
Rabid and riddled with shame,
Playing a game of romantic roulette.

A romantic roulette with yourself,
And the foundation of your identity.

Ali Mansoor (15)
Vyners School, Ickenham

When Fire Reigns

A tranquil night, not a sound seeps through,
The midnight moon illuminates the ground with a grin,
And when calm up above, distress is within,

The ground rumbles, animals flee,
The sky darkens and prepares for what is to be,

The moon disappears in the burning clouds,
And the innocent lives give in to the raging inferno,

The mountain churns, growling in pain,
And what comes next, ash replaces rain,

The blood-curdling liquid runs down the peak,
And engulfs the afraid, the scared, and the weak,

The horror, the fear, was pushed to a halt,
And the sky cleared up and the blazing death stopped,

And all that remained, all that was still,
Were the shrivelled corpses and the charred terrain,

And what followed was a relief to attain.

Bradley Stilwell (11)
Vyners School, Ickenham

Keep Going On

When people are living, we barely see them or give them the time of day,
However, when they die, we can't comprehend that they've left and gone away,
We write out messages, posting how the loss has devastated everyone they knew,
Pretending we were their best friend, acting like we were one of the very few,

The person has passed, so we begin to shed our heartbroken tears,
Sadly, it's more because we never reached out, learning of their fears,
We attend a vigil or a funeral, followed by a wake, to remember their fading light,
Celebrating a dead person who's gone, while never having made things right,

Death is a lesson that teaches, something that shows how short is life,
So always make amends with the living person, ending your trouble and strife,
As, once they're gone, you can think that you're able to say a proper goodbye,
However, the human form is not around, so we talk to a grave or urn, asking why,

We find a picture to put in a frame, get ourselves a tattoo on our arm or chest,
In memory of the one we lost, a dedication to a life that is now at rest,
Convincing ourselves as a comfort that they're now in a better place,
While putting ourselves to sleep remembering their happy smiling face,

Really though, we think to ourselves, did we do enough together before they died?
Were we really there for them? In times they needed us and alone they cried,
We can tell ourselves we were to make us feel better about the life that's gone,
However, really, we know deep inside, we could've helped them keep going on.

Nevaeh Aaliyah Aulakh (12)
Vyners School, Ickenham

I Wish To Be There

There are certain days when I just wish to be there,
The smell of horse goes through my nose,
I wish to be there,
The thought of riding locks into my mind,
I get butterflies in my stomach,
My whole body relaxes.

I wish to be there,
Where dreams can come true,
But many can get hurt,
My eyes glare at the majestic animal
I am lucky enough to be with.

The feeling of sitting in the saddle
Sinks into my mind,
My arms grip on and my legs sit still.

I wish to be there,
When I feel tingles in my spine,
And focus on my bond
With the beautiful animal in front of me.

My mind goes blank,
With only the thoughts of what will happen next,
My posture is still good,
My focus is still on.

The sensation of the horse's movements,
It reminds me of how much I am worth,
It tells me how much I love animals,
It shows me how beautiful nature can really be,
I stay still,
It is the best feeling ever,
I wish I could be there forever.

Natasha Islentsyeva (11)
Vyners School, Ickenham

Goodbyes

Goodbyes are rough
Goodbyes are the worst
Goodbyes are tough
But that my friend, that's just how it works.

Happiness will come
Happiness will end
But who shall know when it's lurking
Will there always be an end?

Goodbyes are hanging up on a call
Goodbyes are saying goodbye to a friend
Goodbyes are when you face loss
But life is not a ball you can just toss.

Goodbyes are rough
Goodbyes are the worst
Goodbyes are tough
But that my friend, that's just how it works.

Be grateful for your happiness
Be grateful of your sorrow
As you can't turn back to yesterday
But you can go forward to tomorrow.

But you can make today the best
As today isn't over just yet
And neither is your life
So carry on making the best.

Ava Queenan (11)
Vyners School, Ickenham

Rupert

Rupert is my fluffy dog,
Although, I think he believes he's a frog,
The way he leaps up in the air,
Where will he land? He just doesn't care.

Rupert has big, brown, friendly eyes,
Staring into them, you can see he is wise,
He uses them to get what he wants,
A cuddle, a sausage, or a butter croissant.

Rupert loves to go out on a walk,
When he sees other dogs, they all hang out and talk,
Whooshing his tail side to side,
Taking every muddy puddle in his stride.

Rupert is the owner of a big, wet nose,
Sniff, sniff, sniff, is how it goes,
Sniffing his way around the house,
Up to my bedroom to sleep as quiet as a mouse.

Rupert is my fluffy dog,
Rupert is my friend,
Rupert will be my friend until the end.

Bobbie Sleet (11)
Vyners School, Ickenham

Fresh Starts

F inally, the last streaks of colour on the canvas,
R eds rich with passion, blue dots of anticipation,
E very colour mixing in harmony with what came before,
S ad greys weave through swirls of joyous yellow,
H ellish blacks course in the places where things got hard.

S tepping back, an artist smiles, remembering
T imes when it was orange, when it was purple, when it was green,
A collection that is now beautiful, no matter what it once seemed,
R eally, it was the ebony clouds that made the yellow so vibrant,
T he artist finishes the canvas, only very slightly blue, and picks up a new one,
S o the first violet strikes of excitement can inspire a brand-new painting.

Ruby Farrington (13)
Vyners School, Ickenham

Awake

Sometimes my mind wakes up before my body,
I open my eyes,
Breathe rapidly and shallow,
My hands grasp at my thighs, trying to rip theirs off mine,

I'm in fight or flight,
But my body is still asleep,
It takes all my strength to stay awake,
I have to life anvils off my eyes,
And push my head off the pillow,
Pushed by memories of its face again,

If I let myself rest,
I will be back there,
Trapped by claws dug underneath his skin,
Suffocated by hands around my throat,
Rays of sun haven't yet reached my window,
But I force my eyes to open,
And keep my head off the pillow,
Staring at my bedroom door of solid wood,

I am safe here,
If I just stay awake.

Amelie Wootton (12)
Vyners School, Ickenham

Bred In Captivity

Never glimpsed its habitat,
Brought for all the world to glare,
The exquisite wildcat.

It doesn't resonate there,
Nor here,
Brought for all the world to glare.

It looks so different from the rest,
It just wants to be with its own,
The exquisite wildcat.

As much as it wants to leave,
It begins to dawn, belonging, but never accepted,
Brought for all the world to glare.

It wants to see the land its ancestors did,
Wants to feel the same Earth beneath its paws,
The exquisite wildcat.

I want to break free,
I have been
Brought for all the world to glare,
The exquisite wildcat.

Sienna Kaur Gill (14)
Vyners School, Ickenham

8000 Miles

I thought 8000 miles was all it took to change my name,
But now I realise, Britain or Ceylon, people are all the same,
I try to get along with everyone I meet,
Some think I'm stupid and some think I'm sweet,
I can hear whispers when I walk down the hall,
They assume I'm a bully because I look intimidating and tall,
Some say I have an attitude, but is being honest supposed to be rude?
The Pearl was a much simpler place, with its warm feeling and ocean waves,
I want to go back, but it isn't really a choice,
So now I'm forced to call this place my home, with my despairing voice.

Shaza Nusrath (15)
Vyners School, Ickenham

Always There

I cannot change the past,
I cannot change the future,
I cannot change my past,
I cannot change my future.

I looked in his eyes,
And I thought,
When a person goes to sleep,
They've just had a tiring life, right?

Every hour of every day,
Every day of every month,
Every month of every year,
I think of him.

I cannot change the past,
I cannot change the future,
I cannot change my past,
I cannot change my future.

Everyone says he has left us,
That's not true,
Though we can't see him, feel him,
He will always be there.

Muhammad Umar Zahid (11)
Vyners School, Ickenham

#ThisGirlCan

T his girl is a powerful athlete,
H er strength is in her speed and skills,
I nside, she is fearful and self-conscious,
S he just wants to be recognised for her achievements,

G oal! She scored another,
I nspired by others who are role models to her,
R unning rapidly through her emotions and feelings,
L earning how to overcome her fears,

C onfidence gained in all her sports,
A chievements start to come flooding in,
N ever again will she hear, "This girl can't." Now it's just, #ThisGirlCan.

Sophie Hawkins (12)
Vyners School, Ickenham

The Days That I Regret

Mesmerising as the stars in the night sky,
Could light up the gloomiest of days,
Overfilled with kindness within her,
Generosity and compassion spread around her,
No amount of words could describe her positivity,

Life without her is losing the warmth of the sun,
Without her, a piece of my heart went,
Even though she is gone, my heart hopes every time I walk in,
I see her, but I am only filled with disappointment and regret,
Every time I look at a picture of her, it just makes me want to pretend it's a nasty nightmare that I'll wake up from.

Shawn Gera (12)
Vyners School, Ickenham

Power Of Books

Have you ever thought about how
To cram a bit more knowledge in that brain?
You don't need to train,
But you need a book to know how to handle a crane.
The library is a place of knowledge,
Or a pathway for college,
Some can teach you how to build a cottage.
Books are the key to imagination,
And to fill that empty storage in the brain.
When you read, there is nothing to lose
And everything to gain.
If you don't like them,
You haven't found the one.
Books are the best place to get
Your questions solved and done.

Ibrahim Ramzan (11)
Vyners School, Ickenham

No Plan B

We're all aware,
But nothing's been done,
Our Planet Earth dying
Is nothing near fun.

Humans still refuse
To clean up the floor,
It's not a joke,
I've seen it happen before.

Let's not forget,
2045,
Who knows if Earth
Will manage to survive?

Everyone says that
We'll live on Mars,
But I promise
We won't make it that far.

This can't continue, it has to stop,
Will Earth be safe for you and me?
Plan A is ruined and there is no Plan B!

Dejonique Wilson (11)
Vyners School, Ickenham

The Bigger Picture

It's been going for so long,
The amount of people dying,
With no reason or cause,
Look at the bigger picture,

Everyone is equal,
There is no need for useless deaths,
Stop the persecution,
Look at the bigger picture,

People need to learn how to change,
It's getting worse day by day,
Value every human's life,
Respect others,
Treat people of colour with respect,

It's been going for so long,
Stop the persecution,
Look at the bigger picture.

Raphael Belai (15)
Vyners School, Ickenham

Winter

Winter's beginning,
In ominous October,
Returns the dark nights,

Trees turning amber,
The golden leaves begin to fall,
Animals retreat,

In November nights,
When all is dark and quiet,
Animals creep out,

All the trees are bare,
And stark against the skyline,
Frost covers the grass,

Darkest December,
When heavy snow starts to fall,
Excitement begins,

In late December,
Fireworks brighten our skies,
All darkness breaks.

Catherine Gallagher (12)
Vyners School, Ickenham

Growing Up

As soon as the fire hit the coffin,
we knew it was final.
Days go by,
my mum's tears flood the house.
We had to be brave,
that's what he would've wanted.

Tears run down my face,
the memories come flooding back.
Every day is filled with pain.
I wish it was me,
I wish it was anyone
but him.

It's been eight years,
I should be over it by now,
but it's impossible.
It broke my family,
it broke me,
I was just a kid.

Juliet Marshall (14)
Vyners School, Ickenham

Cats!

M orning! I said to my cat, then she meowed back,
Y our food is served, I said to my cat,

C utest chunk of fluff, I said to my cat as she rolled around on my bed,
A lways too fast to catch, I said as she ran across the corridor,
T alking about mice? I asked as she spoke to her cat friends,

B eside me every time I sit down,
L icking herself as she calmly sits,
U nder the blanket when I'm sleeping.

Kyle Kohli (12)
Vyners School, Ickenham

School

School, Monday morning,
Waking up heavy and exhausted,
School, a place to learn,
A place where behaviour is the main concern,
School, stressful at times,
Exams, pressure, more and more work assigned,
School, cramming young minds with information,
Six hours a day for learning and education,
School, friendships made and minds displayed,
Hearts broken and the time replayed,
School, a sleepless rhythm,
Sometimes knowledge is better hidden.

Zara Colyer (12)
Vyners School, Ickenham

A Little Spark

In a world where skies are grey,
And hope is lost, with nothing to say,
Where laughter's gone and dreams are rare,
And people live in endless care,
The ruler's hand is heavy and cold,
And freedom's price is far too bold,
No more swings, no more games,
Only sorrow and endless pains,
But still, we hold a little spark
Of hope that shines in the dark,
And we'll keep it burning bright,
Until a better future's in sight.

Daniel Hassanian (15)
Vyners School, Ickenham

Another Day

Just another day,
I opened the door, like every day,
The rocks marking the way,
"Find Baba, he is in the mine," said Ma,
Just another day,
I ran along, jumping across
Each rock as if to play,
I circled the city square,
With other bicycles in disarray,
I looked up and there,
I saw the place I was meant to be,
But, screams of wind,
"Run. Run."
Wearing black, they came,
Just like another day.

Tejpal Chanonia (15)
Vyners School, Ickenham

The Two Doves

The forceful rainclouds above
Flow down on doves that love,

They cry and fly for help,
As seagulls eat their kelp,

The doves find somewhere to hide,
Without needing a trusty guide,

The hawks above watch their prey,
One dove will die today,

As the hawks take their aim,
The dove on the right will go aflame,

The dove on the left got the blame,
Oh, what a shame.

Holly Canovas (12)
Vyners School, Ickenham

My Life In A Zoo

Always in a cage,
Always being watched,
Never seeing beyond the black gates,
Never being free,
Always being looked at with disgust,
Never getting a hug,
Stuck in a cage with nowhere to go,
Feels like jail,
But I must call this home,
My ugly face brings crying eyes,
My scales always bring frightened cries,
Sometimes I wish I was all the way home,
Finally, a place I can call home.

Khwaish Pandya (11)
Vyners School, Ickenham

The Memories Of Islay

Finding a dead crab in an old tin of Spam,
Watching the tide arrive slow and calm,
Building a stepping-stone bridge over a muddy river,
We topple and wobble, each step a quiver,
Hitting a broken, old, torn-bottom boat,
No longer able to float,
Skimming stones which fly,
Sliding the salty air high in the sky.

These are memories I hold close,
Of my bonny Islay on the west coast.

Archie Greenan (11)
Vyners School, Ickenham

The Night Owl

Some may say,
Night rules over the day,
Once we hit the hay,
We have nothing more to say,

The night is calm and makes us weep,
But she has promises to keep,
After sun and lots of sleep,
Sweet dreams come to her cheap,

She rises from her gentle bed,
With thoughts in her head,
"Goodbye, night," she said,
And she went onwards with the day ahead.

Amber Wong (14)
Vyners School, Ickenham

Jaguars

In the distance, a creature with spotted fur,
But hard to see, what a blur,
A predator just there, lying on the grass,
This jaguar, extremely hard to pass,
I saw the jaguar fast asleep,
Yet I still couldn't make a sound, not a peep,
Cautiously is the way that I crept,
At the time, the jaguar slept,
I walked closer, just then,
But he ran away, never to be seen again.

Daniyal Dossa (11)
Vyners School, Ickenham

The Game Of Football

Football, such a wonderful game,
I wake up on a Sunday morning,
Go to the stadium to witness the most incredible game,
The ball, the goal, the crowd,
What an amazing sight!
I love it so much,
Football is where you can really play,
Football might sound easy, but it really isn't,
You see the ball, the players, and sometimes a bee,
Football really is everything to me.

Matthew Parker (11)
Vyners School, Ickenham

Friends

F un you will have together,
R eliable friends who you can trust,
I nside, you cherish the moments you had,
E ndless happiness, endless joy, an end of which there is none,
N o matter what, they will lend a helping hand,
D oing things together, making new memories,
S how you care, don't despair, for they will do the same anywhere.

Munira Khan (11)
Vyners School, Ickenham

Football: WHU Versus Leeds

It's 7:45, let the game begin,
The opponent's box is where we want the ball in,
The night is so cold,
The mighty West Ham need to win and attack,
At the back, we can't be slack,
West Ham need the three points and a win,
Otherwise their manager is heading for the bin,
The game ends 2-2, all square,
I think the result was fair.

Leonardo Sawden (12)
Vyners School, Ickenham

What Am I?

As long as an endless road,
As tiring as a boxing match,
As difficult as an impossible problem,
As regular as the sunrise,
As boring as watching a clock tick,
Homework!

As dark as night,
As light as day,
As enjoyable as a roller coaster,
As melting as wax,
As sticky as honey,
As sweet as sugar,
Chocolate!

Georgina Francis (12)
Vyners School, Ickenham

Golden Galaxy

Up in space where there is no sound,
Looking at the moon so round,

Eight different planets in the solar system,
Each one so very far, but only one is named after a chocolate bar,

Different sizes and colours,
The sun is bigger than all the others,

Even though it may only be a star,
It sends light extremely far.

Deven Daurka (11)
Vyners School, Ickenham

Life Is Like A Daffodil

Life is like a daffodil,
Every year, a new life begins,
Unlike a daffodil, humans make emotions,
Differences and personality,
So if you are to turn a new leaf and start a new life,
Think carefully and from the heart,
Until next year, when you go back to the start,
Because life is like a daffodil,
Whichever way the wind blows.

Nathan Betts (12)
Vyners School, Ickenham

An Eclipse Of Hope

A world was once bright, now dark and grey,
Where hope and joy have flown away,
No laughter echoes in the streets,
Only the sound of shuffling feet.

A ruler rules with a corrupt hand,
No freedom, no choice, no demand,
A dystopia, a world gone wrong,
Where nothing thrives, nothing belongs.

Yara Imad (15)
Vyners School, Ickenham

To The Day

Be awakened to the day,
Knew evil was coming my way,
It was the fault of the greedy,
Women and men, oh so needy,
Work all in dystopia,
Dream none in utopia,
All are too blind to notice
The suffering and injustice,
Soon you will all realise,
And be awakened to the day.

Valentina Cossio-Yates (15)
Vyners School, Ickenham

Malaga, Spain

Malaga, where my heart belongs,
The sun sets upon its beauty as the towns light up,
The sun covers the city like a blanket,
The calm waves overlapping the sand,
The birds singing as the sun sets,
People staying out celebrating until the sunrise,
Malaga, the city of culture and love.

Celina Bandera Villaescusa (12)
Vyners School, Ickenham

Football

F ans are cheering and celebrating,
O utstanding skill from the players,
O ver the goal and into the crowd,
T op of the league,
B alls flying on the pitch,
A ll running and sweating,
L osing matches,
L aughing and loving fans.

Ayrton Rai (12)
Vyners School, Ickenham

Love And Sacrifice

Love is kind,
Love is important,
Love is something for which you have to use your mind,
However, sometimes you have to sacrifice for the ones you love,
Even if it means getting sent to up above,
And that's why showing love is key,
Even if it means not dying peacefully!

Nally Aziz (12)
Vyners School, Ickenham

What She Was

She sat behind the walls of shame,
Lonely as ever could be,
She used to be full of light,
Now only darkness, she knows,
Everyone said it would be alright,
That's the one thing she never felt,
She sat behind her walls of shame,
Wishing nothing would stay the same.

Sophia Monk (12)
Vyners School, Ickenham

Football

F un and a good opportunity,
O utstanding and competitive,
O ptimistic and positive,
T hrilling and exciting,
B est match ever,
A ll about the entertainment,
L eadership and direction,
L oyalty of the players.

Aidan Jones (11)
Vyners School, Ickenham

Shark Poem

S harp teeth made for cutting through flesh,
H ungry and deadly like a tiger,
A ctive and mostly swimming around,
R avenous and carnivorous,
K nife-sharp, its skin feels like sandpaper,
S o fast so that they can catch their prey.

Alexander Baughan (11)
Vyners School, Ickenham

English

E nglish, engaging us in our learning,
N eat writing in our books,
G uaranteed to learn new things,
L earning everything each time,
I ndependent work,
S chool related,
H elping us to understand what our task is.

Michele Cronin (11)
Vyners School, Ickenham

Football Matches

The boys stood,
Eleven on each team,
Ready to show
What a match looks like,
They went to their positions,
And focused on their mission,
Fuelled by their football passion,
But eight of their number
Ended up with a concussion.

Haitao Liang (11)
Vyners School, Ickenham

Football

Fun and competitive,
No matter the weather,
No matter the pain,
A kick always starts the game,
The team must run or pass,
And the opposing team must defend,
90 minutes decide the winner,
You don't want to finish last.

Zoher Alkhouli (12)
Vyners School, Ickenham

Just A Joke

It could be just a joke,
But it still really hurts,
Being made fun of on the spot,
About something you can never change,
You laugh with the others, but it's all fake,
It hurts because it's something you can never change.

Amelia Baah (12)
Vyners School, Ickenham

Family

F ulfil your dreams,
A ssistance and assurance,
M emories and making jokes,
I nfinite love,
L oyalty and laughter,
Y ou only have this one life to enjoy the time spent with the ones you love.

Luca Harrod (12)
Vyners School, Ickenham

World War II

Can't this, can't that,
What can we do?
Fright and fire everywhere,
Wars, suffering,
How can they do this?
No rights and freedom,
Only rules,
Family is all we have now,
But love and warmth are scarce.

Aaron Rashid (12)
Vyners School, Ickenham

Hugo

A companion,
Fur so unique and soft,
Instantly fluffy,

A creature to love,
Running around with joy,
An animal to love,

Leaping to the stars,
More loyal than anything,
My dog named Hugo.

Harvey Matharu (11)
Vyners School, Ickenham

The Five Senses

I can see a clear, bright blue sky,
I can hear the rustling leaves in the atmosphere,
I can feel the cool evening breeze,
I can smell the sweet fragrance of the flowers,
I can taste the ripe, juicy berries of the trees.

Layo Oluyemi (11)
Vyners School, Ickenham

Sport

S port is my favourite thing in the world,
P erfect athlete I want to be,
O r just a dancer,
R unning cross-country, I am very good at,
T hough I may not succeed, I will try my best.

Fleur Wright (12)
Vyners School, Ickenham

My Cat, Derek

D erek is my black and white cat,
E xtremely lazy and loves to nap,
R olls around in the sun,
E njoying the warmth on his tum',
K ind, loyal, and lots of fun.

Matthew Burke (12)
Vyners School, Ickenham

Oh, Wonderful Nature!

Oh, wonderful nature,
With green trees,
And buzzing bees,
The grass is so clean,
And everything is so clean,
The wandering butterflies,
Just make my thoughts fly.

Aaryan Thakrar (12)
Vyners School, Ickenham

The Birds That Chitter-Chatter

Birds are sweet,
Birds are soft,
Birds tweet,
All day long,
Birds chitter-chatter,
Then they come down,
Before the birds' good night rest.

Daniel Gavin (11)
Vyners School, Ickenham

My Bike

I have a bike that is green and black,
I ride it fast and my mum makes me wear a hat,
I ride my bike in the park,
But I am always home before dark.

Harry Deanus (11)
Vyners School, Ickenham

Wars

There's more that goes into winning a war,
Than tanks and planes and guns,
Than men prepared to do their best
To overthrow the Huns.

Sleiman Basma (11)
Vyners School, Ickenham

Young Writers

Young Writers Information

We hope you have enjoyed reading this book – and that you will continue to in the coming years.

If you're the parent or family member of an enthusiastic poet or story writer, do visit our website **www.youngwriters.co.uk/subscribe** and sign up to receive news, competitions, writing challenges and tips, activities and much, much more! There's lots to keep budding writers motivated!

If you would like to order further copies of this book, or any of our other titles, then please give us a call or order via your online account.

Young Writers
Remus House
Coltsfoot Drive
Peterborough
PE2 9BF
(01733) 890066
info@youngwriters.co.uk

Join in the conversation!
Tips, news, giveaways and much more!

YoungWritersUK   YoungWritersCW   youngwriterscw